"Sure you don't want to stay?"

Charlie wasn't sure, not by a long shot. Which made it even more imperative that he go. "I better not."

"Because you're afraid we're violent?" Sarah asked.

"Because. Because of a lot of things. But not that." He hesitated. "There's a lot going on right now and it's complicated."

"Oh."

He hadn't meant to make her feel bad, but they couldn't afford to kid themselves about the truth. He worked for her ex-husband so there couldn't be anything going on between them. End of story.

Dear Reader,

Life doesn't always work out exactly the way we expected. A recent divorce and a startling discovery about her son set Sarah Finley in search of a plan B for her life, which doesn't work out exactly the way she expected, either…it works out better!

I've encountered some unexpected twists of my own. I thought I'd be a veterinarian, instead I became a technical writer, documenting software products, not operating on dogs and cats. In the back of my mind I always thought of being a novelist, but that seemed like the silliest kind of pipe dream. Thanks to the Harlequin Superromance line, I'm living that dream.

For sixty years, Harlequin has been making dreams come true for readers and writers. My mom and I started reading Harlequin books when I was in high school. We've shared so many stories back and forth over the years—I get a special thrill when I put one of my own books in her hands.

I hope you'll enjoy Sarah and Charlie's story. Extras, including behind-the-scenes facts, deleted scenes, and information about previous books, including *The Boyfriend's Back* (about Charlie's older brother), are on my Web site, www.ellenhartman.com. I'd love to hear from you! Send e-mail to ellen@ellenhartman.com.

Ellen Hartman

Plan B: Boyfriend
Ellen Hartman

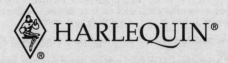

TORONTO • NEW YORK • LONDON
AMSTERDAM • PARIS • SYDNEY • HAMBURG
STOCKHOLM • ATHENS • TOKYO • MILAN • MADRID
PRAGUE • WARSAW • BUDAPEST • AUCKLAND

Recycling programs
for this product may
not exist in your area.

ISBN-13: 978-0-373-71603-6

PLAN B: BOYFRIEND

Copyright © 2009 by Ellen K. Hartman.

www.eHarlequin.com

Printed in U.S.A.

ABOUT THE AUTHOR

Ellen has been making a living as a writer since she graduated from Carnegie Mellon and went to work for Microsoft writing documentation for Word. Currently she lives in a college town in upstate New York where she enjoys writing romances, reading to her kids and persuading her husband to take her out dancing any chance she gets.

Books by Ellen Hartman

HARLEQUIN SUPERROMANCE

1427—WANTED MAN
1491—HIS SECRET PAST
1563—THE BOYFRIEND'S BACK

Don't miss any of our special offers. Write to us at the following address for information on our newest releases.

Harlequin Reader Service
U.S.: 3010 Walden Ave., P.O. Box 1325, Buffalo, NY 14269
Canadian: P.O. Box 609, Fort Erie, Ont. L2A 5X3

This book is dedicated to my online friends, especially the women of the Supers thread on eHarlequin.

Each and every one of you deserves a tiara— you're smart, supportive, generous, and you keep me smiling!

Diana, Harriett, Leslie, Liz, and Mary, my critique partners, read draft after draft and offered substantive comments on everything from properly heroic names to finger foods to serve at strip poker parties.

Thanks for hanging in there with me.

CHAPTER ONE

SARAH FINLEY EXAMINED herself carefully in the mirror on the back of the closet door in her front hall. The gleaming walnut woodwork surrounding the mirror provided a dark counterpoint to her "hip, yet involved and respectable mother" outfit—a knee-length charcoal skirt with a slight flare at the hem to soften it; crisp, white shirt patterned with pale pink circles from the newest Talbot's catalog; and a cropped black knit jacket with chunky, artistic buttons.

She was debating about the abstract print scarf. If she wore the scarf would it say "I'm taking this issue seriously" or "I've just come from shopping"? She'd never faced this situation before, wasn't confident she was approaching it correctly. She seriously doubted, however, if even Emily Post knew the exact dress code for meeting with the school principal to discuss the possible expulsion of your first-grader.

Sarah bit back a semihysterical laugh. She couldn't allow that laugh. Not now. That laugh had burst out inappropriately with increasing frequency ever since Erik left her eight months ago. For a while she'd thought she was managing. But the repeated appearance of the laugh and its distressing tendency to morph into a sob made her wonder just how well she was coping. Not well, she was beginning to suspect.

Which was bad.

Because Sarah was a coper. It was her claim to fame. Her hallmark. It was why she was always the vice-president or the volunteer coordinator rather than the president of groups like the PTA, the pool association, even the block-party committee. She fit in, she managed, she coped. Sarah Finley could cope with anything.

Except, apparently, her husband's infidelity, her resulting divorce, and the fact that Simon, her well-loved if perplexing six-year-old, was in danger of being chucked out of Carol Ryan Memorial Elementary before he'd mastered alphabetical order.

Sarah ripped the scarf off her neck and stuffed it into her mouth in a vain attempt to stifle the laugh. Which did turn into a sob. Which she was only able to control by thinking of Simon. Her baby. Currently in lockdown in the principal's office on what Jessica Jordan, the school secretary, had ever so sweetly informed her was a weapons violation.

Oh, Simon.

Sarah dropped the scarf, grinding it under one tasteful black sling-back as she headed out of the house.

WHEN SHE OPENED THE DOOR of Carol Ryan Memorial Elementary, she was met with the smells of kids and books and school lunches, familiar from her years of volunteering, but she was too nervous to find them comforting. Although her hands were shaking slightly, she managed to hang on to her self-control until she was startled into a shriek when her nine-year-old daughter, Lily, darted out from the girls' bathroom.

"Mom! What are you doing here?" Lily asked with enough obviously fake surprise to sink any attempt at subterfuge.

"I could ask you the same thing," Sarah said. But she didn't need to ask. Lily had been born with the type of sophisticated social radar many a Statlerville matron would have killed for. Of course she'd heard about whatever it was her little brother had done.

Lily held on to the door frame as she peered behind Sarah and then pulled herself back upright. "Going to spring Simon?"

"Please, Lily, go back to class."

Lily stood uncertainly, glancing from her mother to the door of the school. "Okay. But are you alone?"

"We'll talk when you get home," Sarah said before pressing a kiss on top of her daughter's blond hair and turning her toward the fourth-grade hallway. Once she was certain Lily was on her way back to class—no need to add truancy to the Finley troublemaking column today— Sarah took a deep breath and headed for the office.

Jessica Jordan looked up from her desk, and when she saw Sarah, cupped her hand around the receiver and whispered, "She's here. I'll call you back."

At least, Sarah thought, she'd made an attempt to cover up the fact that she was leaking the incident faster than a government staffer with an open line to FOX News. Since Erik moved in with the Snake in the Grass formerly known as Lauren Smiley, aka His Boss, the

Statlerville grapevine had been fed a steady diet of Information about the Finley Situation. Simon's transgression was just the latest in a long string of stories.

"Sarah. How nice to see you. I mean…" Jessica, never anyone's candidate for Most Socially Adept, fumbled. Obviously school secretary training did not include a segment on how to greet last year's Tip Top PTA Volunteer on the occasion of a weapons infraction by her son.

"Where's Simon?" Sarah asked.

"In with Ted." Jessica punched a button on the phone and leaned over the speaker to say, "Mrs. Finley is here."

She nodded toward the inner office door and Sarah moved forward. She'd gone straight through school with Jessica, and she'd never known the other woman to be actively mean. She liked to gossip, sure, but she wouldn't have said that, said "*Mrs.* Finley," just to rub it in that Sarah was here alone and Erik was in Bermuda on a yacht with His Boss. Would she? Sarah felt the bad laugh coming again, but she stifled it.

She needed to keep her thoughts here because none of that other stuff mattered. What *did* matter was Simon and what Sarah would need to do to spring him, thank you very much, Lily.

She pulled open the office door, expecting to see her son dejected or terrified. Angry would have been more understandable than what she did see—excited? Simon was perched on the edge of a wooden chair, his sneakers curled around the rungs, and the look in his bright blue eyes was exactly the same one he wore on Christmas morning before he tore into the presents.

"Simon?" she asked, wondering if somehow Jessica had mixed up the message. Maybe he wasn't in trouble. Sure, he'd had kind of a rocky start to his school career and his performance in first grade so far hadn't been stellar. But that could have changed. Maybe he'd won an award—best reader or best listener—heck, at this point she'd take best scissors operator if it meant he hadn't…

"Sarah, I'm sorry to have to call you," Ted Bryant, the principal, said as he rose to greet her.

Simon looked from her to the door, his bright expression flagging. "Where's Dad?" he asked.

Sarah ignored him for the moment. Wherever Erik and Lauren were, it didn't matter to this discussion. The important thing was clearing this up and getting Simon back to class. She focused on Ted's lean, angular face. He'd been a rower in college, and it still showed in the defined planes of his body and the slight tilt to his posture. She sat in the chair next to Simon, not looking at the empty seat, which was clearly meant for the other parent, and prepared to hear the details and then cope with them.

Ted started with "carving knife," moved through "threatening gesture," and was starting in on "serious consequences" when she had to stop him. Simon had gradually shifted forward in his chair, his eyes fixed on the door as his sneakers swung gently back and forth. With the softly curling brown hair and blue eyes he'd inherited from Erik, he looked every inch the adorable, lovable little boy whose face she'd washed that morning.

Had the knife been in his backpack while she'd put the double knots in his size-one Nikes? Somehow, something was seriously wrong. Sarah Finley's children were normal, ordinary suburban Philadelphia students getting an expensive private-school education from what was supposed to be the premier school in their district. Her children did not introduce weapons to the first-grade classroom. If she was going to get this sorted, she needed facts.

"Simon, why would you take a knife out of the house? You could have hurt yourself or someone else."

Ted leaned forward. "That's the reasoning behind the zero tolerance."

"I don't mean that he'd do it on purpose, Ted. Please. He's a six-year-old child, not some miniature hit man." She turned back to her son. "The knife could have cut through your backpack and really hurt someone. What were you thinking?"

"Where's Dad?" Simon repeated, his tone less hopeful, edging into stubborn.

"Sarah, we have a lot to discuss, but I'm not sure you understand. Zero tolerance means he's suspended. You'll have a disciplinary hearing within five days to review the options, which range from no further action straight up to expulsion. Simon's been having enough problems fitting in here. After this…you need to prepare yourself."

Suspended hit her like a slap in the face right before *expulsion* landed like a rock in her gut, and then *Simon's problems* cut the legs out from under her. Ted was serious. But surely there were contingencies, ways that children with the proper explanations were allowed to circumvent…what had he called it? Zero tolerance?

"Ted—" she started, but Simon interrupted her.

"Where's Dad?"

Maybe she hadn't heard Ted right? Would he really suspend Simon, her Simon, for something that was clearly a mistake? She knew that Simon's teacher had issues with his behavior in class and that he didn't seem to be exactly fitting in perfectly. But he was Simon. Not someone who needed to be expelled.

He tugged her sleeve and she looked at him. Okay. One thing at a time. She answered Simon more to feel like she was accomplishing something than because she cared about Erik's whereabouts. "Simon, you know Dad's on a trip."

"No. Lily said if I brought the knife to school you'd come *together.* She said if it was big trouble, Dad would come, and we made sure it was the *big* knife, so where is he?"

"Lily said…" Ted began before looking away. Sarah felt renewed hope. He really was a kind man. Considerate. Please God, discreet. Now that they'd gotten to the root cause, things could be cleared up. Lily had quite a lot to answer for, but under the circumstances, they must be back to a sane place where this would be treated like the first-grade error it was. Good for a laugh, not suspension.

But then Ted spoke again, and instead of explanations, he'd homed in on conspiracies. Ted pegged Lily as the mastermind and as such she could no longer be tolerated at Carol Ryan Memorial Elementary, either. He was surprised that a student of her caliber would be involved in this behavior, but he once again invoked zero tolerance, this time for inciting violence. He was very sorry. Very matter-of-fact.

He was also very mistaken if he thought Sarah was going to listen to him malign her children for one more second.

Afterward, she congratulated herself on her control. Sarah hadn't gouged Ted's kind eyes out with her French-manicured fingernails. She hadn't whacked him with one of his rowing trophies. She hadn't even raised her voice. She'd merely stood and tucked Simon's hand into her own. Picking the knife up off Ted's desk, she'd examined it briefly. It was the large carving knife from the set Aunt Deirdre had given her at her bridal shower ten years ago.

"I imagine you'll need this as evidence," she'd said before she jammed it point down into a stack of pink tardy notices on Ted's desk. The knife was still quivering in the wood as she stalked out of the office to collect Lily from her fourth-grade classroom.

Ted had kept talking to her and she'd kept ignoring him while Lily unwisely protested about a test that afternoon. She explained in an exceedingly calm voice that they were leaving immediately and she didn't care if the test was an entrance exam for *Harvard,* Lily had ten seconds to get her backpack and *come with her now*.

All in all, Carol Ryan Memorial Elementary had gotten off easy. One useless, rule-bound administrator's desk suffering one stab wound was nothing, nothing when weighed against the rage she felt.

The children sat white-faced and silent in the back of her Volvo SUV. She didn't miss that they were crammed together into the farthest seat, leaving the middle one empty. *Wonderful*. She'd terrified her own offspring. That only added to her anger.

Not at Simon. Not at Lily. Not even at Ted Bryant or the imbecile who'd invented the concept of zero tolerance. No. She was rational enough to aim the full force of blame exactly where it belonged. At Erik. Former husband. Father of her criminal brood. Root of all evil.

Erik wasn't in town. She knew that. He was somewhere off Bermuda on Lauren's yacht, celebrating. Sipping Cristal, no doubt, while he snuggled up to the Snake in the Grass and…*ew*. She did not need to imagine what they were doing together.

Sarah was clear on just one thing at the moment. Erik needed to pay. He needed to pay right now. And since he was out of reach, she turned the car toward the investment firm of Baxter Smiley. Founded by Robert B. Baxter, currently run by his great-great-granddaughter, Lauren Smiley, Baxter Smiley handled the portfolios of high net worth individuals and families looking for a discreet investment firm with an impeccable track record. Luckily the firm's services also included a kind security guard named Donny who would watch her children while she "popped upstairs."

She didn't wait for the elevator. The beat of her shoes chanted *Baxter Smiley, Baxter Smiley* as she ran up the stairs.

Erik was a senior partner. The firm provided his income, his stature in the community and, she'd recently found out, a revolving pool of junior associates for Erik to…*ew*. And, of course, it had provided Lauren. His Boss. Soon, if she read the signs right, to be his new wife.

Yes, Sarah thought, as she reached the fifth floor. If Erik and Lauren were unavailable to answer for their crimes, she would find someone else who could. Baxter Smiley was the diseased root of everything wrong with her life, and she was ready to reap some satisfaction. She deserved a little something special today, anyway. It wasn't every day a girl received her final divorce decree on her tenth wedding anniversary.

CHARLIE LIKED HIS OFFICE door closed. Especially these past two weeks. With Erik and Lauren gone, and, *goddamn,* he still couldn't believe that had played out the way it had, it was like the rest of the firm had gone giddy. Which was saying something, because Baxter Smiley was normally much closer to morgue quiet than giddy. He hated to think who might be following Lauren and Erik's example—messing around with your co-workers was wrong in too many ways for him to count.

So he kept the door closed. The crazy stayed out in the hall and he got his work done. Today it seemed like the crazy was louder than usual, though. If Lauren didn't get her cheating ass back to town soon, she was going to have trouble reining her staff back in.

For himself, he'd be happy if she stayed away one more week. That would give him time to seal the Ryan deal. He was inches from convincing Henry Ryan Senior to transfer his account to Baxter Smiley. Where Senior went, Junior and his two brothers went, along with their five combined ex-wives, whom Senior still counted as family. Charlie tugged on the knot of his silk tie and then impatiently straightened it. If he scored the Ryan family, that would clinch his promotion to partner.

When he scored the Ryan family.

He glanced down at the leather portfolio on his desk. It contained every bit of information he'd been able to dig up on Senior. He flipped the pages until he found the time line he'd created before he made the first contact. Before he'd even started lobbying for a seat on the Carol Ryan Memorial Elementary board, which was where he'd befriended Junior, who'd introduced him to Senior. It had taken most of a year, but he was finally *that* close.

What the hell was up with the noise? It sounded as if someone was screaming out there. How was he supposed to work in this atmosphere?

Crash.

That wasn't high spirits because the boss was out of town. That was a vase or possibly a potted plant meeting a violent end on the parquet floors of the Baxter Smiley foyer. His parents had tossed enough pottery at each other in his childhood that he recognized the sound effects. Come to think of it, the shouting sounded familiar enough to make him wonder if his mom had come back from the grave. If she had, it would be typical for her to show up throwing stuff at his office while he was trying to work.

Another crash. Charlie couldn't stand it. He stalked out from behind his desk and flung the door open. A crowd was gathered at the end of the hall, at the door to the foyer.

At Baxter Smiley, they were good at what they did— their clients came in rich and got richer the longer they stayed. But along with the professional reputation came the illusion created by the offices that everything and everyone connected with the firm was genteel, man-nered and worthy of admission into the club. Didn't matter which club, just that it was clear in everyone's mind there was no standard so exclusive that Baxter Smiley couldn't meet it.

This illusion involved a lot of hardwood, a lot of designer fabrics from Europe and art. Real art. Which, if he wasn't mistaken, was currently being smashed piece by piece in the foyer.

Charlie pushed through the crowd of his coworkers until he could see the lobby. Then he understood why no one seemed capable of dealing with the problem. The problem wasn't a *what*. It was a *who*. Sarah Finley. The scorned wife. Sure, he'd wanted to kill Erik and Lauren for what they'd done and all the upheaval it had caused at the firm. But judging from the way Sarah was tossing vases, he'd have to get in line.

Malcolm Donnelly, one of the senior partners, a colleague of Erik's just under Lauren at the top of the Baxter Smiley organizational chart, was standing near the front of the crowd, panicked, his face red. "Charlie, thank God. Stop her."

Sarah picked up a potted jade and dropped it from shoulder height to the floor. "You're the senior partner," Charlie protested. "You stop her."

"You know her. I don't."

True. He knew Sarah Finley. Knew her the same way all the kids who went to St. Peter's Elementary and then high school knew one another eventually. The way a guy knows his brother's wife's best friend. The way a person who danced with another person one night at a homecoming dance back in high school, knew… *Screw it.* Fine. He knew her.

He strode toward the desk where Madison, the bright-eyed, fresh-out-of-college receptionist, was clearly overwhelmed. Sarah looked normal enough. She was dressed in a sharp little jacket and her blond hair was pulled back in a black leather headband, but her eyes were shooting sparks. The ground around her feet was littered with broken pieces of…just about everything breakable that five minutes before had been creating an old-world ambience in the foyer.

With her eyes on Madison, Sarah said in a tight voice, "I want to speak to Erik. I want you to locate him for me. Now." Sarah had what seemed to be the last intact vase from the foyer display of Craftsman art in her hand. Madison's voice shook as she tried to calm Sarah down.

"Mrs. Finley—" she started but gasped when Sarah interrupted.

"I told you not to call me that." She threw the vase. Charlie barely managed to grab it as it sailed toward his face. He lifted the vase with what he hoped was a disarming smile. He'd spent years studying his brother, JT, for whom disarming was second nature. Charlie, the younger McNulty, had always had to work harder at it, but he was pretty sure he'd perfected it. JT might be charming, but Charlie was diligent. Sarah's anger wobbled in the face of his nonconfrontational, doggedly disarming smile. She lifted a hand and said, "Hello, Charlie." But then she was right back at Madison, who appeared ready to throw up.

"Where. Is. My. Husband?" She picked up a heavy marble bookend. Madison's throat worked as she tried to swallow, but it didn't look like she had a whole lot of luck.

"Mrs. Fin—"

Charlie was around the desk and had caught Sarah's hand before she could let the bookend fly. Madison might have a degree in business administration from Columbia, but it was clear she'd flunked "Listening to the Madwoman 101." Fortunately for her, Charlie was well versed in that topic. Either of the McNulty brothers could have taught that class with their eyes closed.

"She would like you to call her Sarah," he said gently, as he continued to hold Sarah's arm with just enough pressure so she would know he wasn't fooling around. Vases were one thing, but bookends could cause a real injury.

"Thank you," Sarah said. She dropped her arm, letting the bookend fall onto the leather chair next to her. "Finally, someone who can follow a simple direction."

Madison opened her mouth, but Charlie silenced her with a slight head shake. He could handle this. He'd joined Baxter Smiley on purpose, because it seemed like one of the last places *this* would happen, but he hadn't forgotten his childhood.

"Maybe I can help you out, Sarah?" he asked.

"I would like someone in this miserable establishment to tell me where I can find my husband. You have contact information. She wouldn't have left her precious business without letting you know how to contact her."

Charlie winced. Sarah knew about Erik and Lauren, of course. Everyone knew she knew. Erik wasn't circumspect and the divorce must be close to done. But Charlie hadn't expected to actually have to talk to her about it. About them. Good Lord. He should have kept his office door closed.

"How about this? Let's head back to my office.…" He saw the press of Baxter Smiley employees gawking from the doorway. He couldn't make her run that gauntlet. He needed to defuse the situation. Remove the bomb from the premises. "Or better yet, can I drive you home?"

"I'm not leaving until I…" Sarah shook her head as if she couldn't remember where she was. The adrenaline high of her anger was fading. She looked from him to Madison and then scuffed the toe of her black shoe through the mess at her feet. "I would like to know where Erik is," she said quietly. "That's what I would like."

That was a little better. She'd lost her momentum and now they were dealing with remorse. Less dangerous physically, but still unpredictable. He needed to get her out of here. Later he would kill Lauren and Erik for bringing this crap into Baxter Smiley. Sarah might be the one breaking vases, but he knew who'd thrown the first punch. Still, Sarah was the issue now.

Charlie put his hands gently on her shoulders. He could feel her trembling through the knit of her jacket. Her blue eyes were clouded with pain and bewilderment. *God, this sucked.* He willed her to pay attention to him. If he could get her trust, he could get her moving. "I'll find the information you need. Okay? But let's head on out of here. These people have work they need to do. Let's let them do it."

As he'd hoped, his mentioning the audience brought them to her awareness. She paled as she saw how many people were staring at them. "Fine."

He could see her gathering her dignity. Straighten the spine. Lift the chin. That little pat women gave their purses when they were setting out. Good for her, Charlie thought grudgingly. She might have just put on the biggest display of batshit crazy ever witnessed by the refined halls of Baxter Smiley, but at least she was going out with style.

He held out his arm and Sarah took it lightly. He led her through the art carnage toward the elevator. "Madison, forward any calls to my cell, right?"

He didn't hear her reply, but he assumed she'd heard him. Charlie couldn't worry about that just then, anyway, though, because if he wasn't mistaken, Sarah Finley was fighting a losing battle to hold in a mother lode of tears. *Perfect.*

Ten minutes ago he'd been mapping out his endgame for roping one filthy-rich old guy and all his filthy-rich relatives into the Baxter Smiley corral. Now he was dealing with a soon-to-be-crying woman. Thanks to his mother, he was not without experience in this area, either. But also thanks to his mother, crying women were the exact women he took greatest pains to avoid. Charlie hated irony.

He thought about backing off, finding someone to do this instead of him. But there wasn't anyone here now he trusted.

Screw it. Erik and Lauren had caused this, but now that it was on his plate, it couldn't be helped.

CHAPTER TWO

THE ANCIENT ELEVATOR arrived with a clank of gears. The outer door opened and he leaned around Sarah to pull the inner cage door open. When they were in, he pulled the inner door closed and pressed the button. He patted her hand as the outer doors closed and they started for the lobby. "Hang in there, Sarah. You can do this. One step at a time."

She still hadn't started crying by the time they reached the lobby, and he was so focused on hoping he might be able to get her in her car and be done with the whole thing that he almost didn't notice her kids.

But all of a sudden they were there, standing next to the reception desk, with Donny, the security guard, staring curiously from him and Sarah to the kids.

"Mom?" Lily said. "Are we going now?"

Sarah turned away and the choked noise she made was definitely a stifled sob. He gave her points for trying to hide it, but at the same time, he realized it was teeming rain outside and his hopes sank. He wasn't getting out of this anytime soon. No way was he letting Sarah get behind the wheel with her kids in the car in this kind of weather when she was in this kind of shape.

He didn't want her kids to see if she went nuts again when he told her his plan. He scanned the lobby quickly, looking for a place they could talk privately, but the kids were standing with Donny, and a pair of women he recognized as doctors from the practice on the third floor were sitting in the only chairs. The rest of the lobby was open, no chance of a private moment.

Who the hell designed this lobby, anyway?

Sarah pressed the heels of both hands against her eyes as if she could hold the tears in that way.

"You know what," he said. "Sarah, I have the information you need, but it's over here." He made eye contact with Donny. "Watch the kids for a second. We'll be right back."

He put one arm around Sarah to steer her toward the restrooms on the opposite end of the lobby. She felt tiny against his side. He hadn't realized how short she was. She usually carried herself with such energy, he guessed her height, or lack of it, had never really registered.

When he got promoted to senior partner, his first project was going to be adding an office down here for emergencies like this, but for now, if he wanted privacy, he had two choices. Men's or ladies'. He pushed the ladies' room door open and pulled Sarah inside.

She stopped short as soon as the door swung shut behind them. "What are you doing, Charlie?"

"I'm giving you a few seconds to pull yourself together before we go back out there where your children are."

"Leave my children out of this."

Yeah. Because he'd been the one who dragged them

into it. For that matter, he'd have been perfectly happy to leave himself out of it, too. But it didn't seem likely any of them were going to get what they wanted anytime soon.

"Listen, Sarah, it's pouring rain and you're upset. I don't want you to drive."

"I'm fine." She had black mascara smudges under each eye. Her voice was shaky with tears, and the black headband that was supposed to be holding her hair back was inching forward. Sarah was a lot of things right then, but "fine" was demonstrably not one of them. He didn't like seeing anyone in distress, but it seemed doubly bad on Sarah. Her usual sparkle was gone, and as he watched her wilt even more, his anger at Erik grew. This was all wrong.

Without really thinking, he put a hand on either side of the headband and slid it back into place. She closed her eyes and leaned into his right hand as if his touch were comforting to her. He opened his palm and pressed it on the side of her curls and then withdrew it. Weepy women tended to turn clingy. He didn't have time for clingy.

He grabbed a few paper towels from the dispenser and handed them to her. "I don't want to get into an argument with you. You look like you've had about enough today. But you're not feeling right. Your kids are little. It's pouring outside. I'd like to drive you home."

Sarah held the paper towels to her face. "I'm sorry," she said.

"Let's get you home."

Sarah nodded and sniffed behind the paper towels. "All right."

Just then the door swung open and the doctors from

the lobby came in. The taller one in the front, Kimberly Something, stopped so suddenly her smaller, dark-haired friend ran into the back of her.

"We need a minute here, please," he said, hoping they wouldn't recognize him.

"Charlie?" Kimberly said. "This is a surprise."

Her friend peered around her. "Did he go in the wrong door on purpose? That *is* you, isn't it, Sarah?"

"I don't know," Kimberly said. "He's in the ladies' room for *some* reason. What are you doing in here?"

That was an excellent question and one he was sure he was going to be asking himself for days to come.

They tried to look around him to Sarah, but he shielded her with his body. Good thing she was short. He wasn't buying their fake surprise for a second. "Just washing my hands. The sink in the men's room is broken."

They looked doubtful. "Really?" Kimberly said. They waited.

The dark-haired one let the door half close to look at the outside of it and said, "They should put a sign on the door."

"Yes, they should," he agreed.

They stood. He stood. Sarah sniffed. More standing. Oh, hell, they weren't leaving, and no amount of uncomfortable silence was going to make them. He tried to get Sarah moving toward the door, but she resisted.

"You promised you'd give me his number," Sarah said, oblivious to the pair standing in the doorway.

Charlie counted to five in his head and then gave the doctors JT's disarming smile. At the sight of it, they pressed closer together in the doorway and exchanged a nervous look. He had the idea his "disarming" had stopped working.

He pulled out his cell phone and scrolled through the contacts until he found the number Lauren had given him but made him swear he would share with no one and would delete as soon as she came back. He read it to Sarah, who typed it into her phone but didn't make the call. *Thank God for small favors.* He'd bet good money that whatever Sarah wanted to say to Erik was going to be loud with a side of hysterical. He hoped to be far away when she made that call.

He was ready to leave again when she sniffed and blew her nose in the paper towels. "Don't you want to know what's wrong?"

No. No, he really did not. The doctors edged a few steps closer.

"If you want to tell me, you can go ahead," he said.

Anything, as long as they could get the hell out of the ladies' restroom.

She crumpled up the paper towels and shot them toward the wastebasket but missed. "Simon and Lily got suspended from school. They can no longer be tolerated among the other children because Simon is potentially violent and Lily—" She pulled in a deep breath. "Lily is a criminal mastermind."

One of the doctors gasped behind him and the other one shushed her.

Sarah started to brush past them, but Kimberly put a hand on her arm.

"You poor thing, Sarah. I'm sure this is all a big

mistake," she said with enough open curiosity in her voice it was clear she was hoping for more details.

"Well, Kimberly, it was certainly a big knife." Sarah let out a crazy laugh and left the room.

In the silence that followed, he leaned down and picked up the towels and threw them in the can. Then he squeezed past Kimberly and her friend, although they were pressed so far against the wall after Sarah's revelation that he didn't really have to squeeze. Did they think he had the big knife on him? He could feel their eyes on his back as he crossed the lobby.

Donny leaned on the counter, watching as Sarah grabbed her kids by the hands. Charlie thought about trying the disarming thing again on the guard, but since he felt more uptight than he had been in years, he guessed it would only backfire. He'd bring the man a bottle of Scotch tomorrow. In a situation like this, bribes were more effective than any stupid smile.

It turned out she'd parked her SUV right outside the doors and left the engine running. He was impressed with her foresight until he saw she'd also left the driver-side door open. Not foresight, then, but blind anger. A puddle had formed on the front seat.

None of the Finleys spoke to him as they climbed one after the other into the back. He stared at the puddle, but it didn't dry up or even shrink. He was getting drenched standing outside the car, so he brushed as much of the water as he could off the seat before he resigned himself and got in. His ass and thighs were immediately soaked, and he asked himself what else could go wrong as he headed for Sarah's house.

The quiet from the backseat made him nervous, and his attention was divided between the road and the rearview mirror. Sarah wasn't crying anymore and he gave her credit for that. Lily was sitting perfectly straight, her backpack in her lap. She kept sneaking glances at her mom. Eventually she whispered, "I'm sorry."

Sarah picked up her daughter's hand and held it. "You're fine," she murmured.

Simon was focused on Charlie. The boy's expression was calm, his soft hair hanging in his face in damp waves. Was that the face of a violent person? He looked like a fairly normal kid to Charlie, but who knew? He hadn't spent much time with the Finley kids beyond seeing them at his brother's house once in a while, since his sister-in-law, Hailey, and Sarah were best friends, or at some events for the firm.

"You went in the girls' room," Simon said. "I saw you."

Charlie nodded. "Just for a second."

"It was four minutes and twenty-eight seconds. I have a stopwatch." He held up his wrist to show off a thick black diver's-style watch.

Charlie decided he wouldn't contest the timing question. The kid would make a good lawyer.

"Boys shouldn't go in the girls' room. Not even just to see what's different in there," Simon said carefully. "That's a way you get in trouble." He clearly spoke from experience.

Sarah put her arm around her son and he leaned into her. Charlie looked away quickly, back to the road in front of him. His wallet was getting wet in his back pocket, so he pulled it out and dropped it on the passenger seat. As he did, he noticed that the packet of papers lying there was Sarah and Erik's divorce decree. *Jesus.* He hoped that hadn't come through just today. He checked the mirror again and Sarah was watching him, her mascara-streaked face rigid.

SARAH SAT IN THE BACK of her own car, one arm around each of her children, and tried to figure out exactly what had happened. The day was fuzzy, unreal. She remembered getting dressed to go to the school and she remembered talking to Ted, but after that…she wasn't sure of the details and the things she did think she remembered, well…judging from the look on Charlie McNulty's face, she had gone insane. Worse, she was pretty sure he felt sorry for her.

She tightened her hold on the kids. She had to get it together. Charlie was taking her home, and once they were there she was sure she'd feel better. She'd feed the kids something warm and wholesome. Maybe oatmeal with raisins and a pat of organic butter. Then she'd get them ready for bed, and maybe after that she could figure out how her life had gotten so out of control.

Charlie pulled around to the back of her house, and Sarah helped the kids run up on the patio while she dug through her purse. Charlie came up behind them and held her keys out. Of course. He'd been driving.

"Thanks," she said. "I'd invite you in, but, well, it's not a good time. I…I appreciate your help."

She pushed the kids ahead of her and went inside, so happy to be back, she couldn't even force herself to be polite to Charlie. She'd apologize tomorrow. As soon as she'd sorted herself and the kids out, she'd make sure she told him how sorry she was. She'd make sure he knew she was just fine.

CHARLIE WATCHED HER USHER the kids inside and turn the lights on, and then he looked out at her car. His own car was back in the parking lot at Baxter Smiley. He could walk there. It would take him about an hour, and in the rain he'd probably contract pneumonia. If he did, he was going to make sure JT sent the bill for the funeral directly to Erik Finley.

Charlie pulled out his phone. He didn't care what Sarah had said about being fine and needing to be alone. She needed reinforcements. And he needed a ride home.

Fifteen minutes later, JT's black MG pulled into the driveway behind Sarah's Volvo. JT got out and then held an umbrella open while he helped his wife, Hailey, out of the passenger side. Hailey was tall, and under normal circumstances, utterly graceful and poised. In the last few weeks of her pregnancy, she'd become ungainly and had developed an alarmingly bad temper as a result. JT held her arm as they came up the stairs, Hailey's seventeen-year-old daughter, Olivia, behind them.

"What's going on, Charlie?" Hailey asked.

"Why are you standing out here?" JT asked.

"Hey, Uncle Charlie. You're all wet," Olivia said.

Despite not being a blood relative, Charlie was convinced Olivia had inherited her sense of humor from his dad. "Nice to see you, kid," he said as he ignored her parents.

Hailey pushed the door open and stepped into the kitchen. "Get in here," she said.

"No," Charlie protested. "JT's driving me home. I'm soaked."

"You're not going anywhere until you tell me what's been happening," Hailey said. "Start talking."

Sarah must have heard them because she came back around the corner into the kitchen. When she saw them, she let out a little shriek. As soon as she realized who it was, though, she said, "Oh, Hailey."

Hailey crossed the kitchen faster than a woman of her bulk should be able to move and put her arms around Sarah. Charlie heard the crying start and he edged toward the back door.

"Either give me your keys or take me home now," he said to JT. His brother tore his eyes away from Sarah and Hailey.

"You're not leaving me here with them."

"What a pair of chickens," Olivia said in disgust.

"Chicken and smart aren't necessarily mutually exclusive," Charlie said as he backed out the door.

SARAH LET HERSELF FALL apart, choking out disjointed pieces of the story against Hailey's collar. Her face got hot, and she knew she was squeezing her friend too hard, but it felt so good to have someone to lean on after so many months of holding it together.

"Sarah," Hailey murmured in her ear. "Sarah, stop."

At the same moment she felt a small hand on her hip. "Mom?"

It was Simon.

"Mom, Lily and I decided I should write a note just like I did when I climbed into the Do Not Touch part to get a better look at the bones on the field trip and the lady at the museum made me sit outside. When you're finished crying, would you help me spell *knife?*"

Sarah kept her face hidden against Hailey while she took a deep breath. She wanted nothing as much as to let it all out, but she couldn't. Her children were here and Erik was not and that meant she was the parent they had. As bad as her day had been, theirs had been pretty rough, too, and she needed to pull herself together and be their mother.

She could do this.

Sarah Finley was a coper, right? Well, this was just one more situation, albeit a colossally messed-up situation, for her to cope with.

JT GRABBED A TOWEL OUT OF the trunk of his car and made Charlie sit on it. "My wife has to ride in that seat later, man. I can't have you dripping all over it."

"Fine," Charlie said. What was another indignity or two to cap off this freaking fantastic day?

"Where to? Your car or your place?"

"Car's at work. I need to change."

"Right."

JT pulled the car around and drove out of Sarah's driveway. The rain beat on the windshield, and the wipers weren't doing much good to wash it away.

"You going to tell me what the hell is going on?"

"Sarah had some kind of fit. It was like she took lessons from Mom." Charlie hated thinking about it.

When he was a kid, his parents' marriage had been volatile. His mom wasn't happy unless she was involved in drama. If she couldn't find some, she'd make it. His dad was almost always ready to go with her, riding his quick temper into some truly epic scenes.

Charlie had hated every minute of it. As soon as possible, he'd moved out and since then had done his best to make sure his life was drama-free. Seeing Sarah, a woman he respected, someone he'd always liked, acting nuts, had thrown him for a loop. It was as if she'd broken ranks. Once someone like Sarah Finley crossed that kind of line, it made it seem that much easier for someone like him to get pulled across, too. With his family history, he worried that it was only a matter of time, anyway.

"I don't know what precipitated it, but she showed up at the office and wrecked the lobby. She was chucking vases and smashing pots and all I can tell is she wanted to find Erik."

"Sarah was smashing things in the lobby at Baxter Smiley?"

"Look, JT, believe me or don't, that's what happened. I know a smashed vase when I see one." He definitely knew a woman losing control when he saw one.

"I'm sure she had a reason."

"Yeah. She was pissed. That dick Erik. Their divorce is final and he's off in Bermuda somewhere with Lauren celebrating. He didn't leave Sarah any way to contact him."

"I didn't know the divorce came through."

Charlie let out his breath. "I think it came today. I saw the papers in her car."

"God, no wonder she flipped."

Charlie thought back on what she'd said. "I'm not sure if it was the divorce. Is that little kid of hers normal?"

"Simon?"

"Yeah."

"He's kind of intense, but he's six. Kids that age are all out there in their own ways."

Charlie watched the rain drip down the window of the car. "I'm pretty sure he got expelled. Brought a knife to school?" Saying it out loud made it seem even harder to believe, but just because none of it made sense didn't mean it hadn't happened.

JT made the turn onto Charlie's street too fast. "Simon? That's ridiculous. He's still in first grade."

"I guess," Charlie said. But he remembered the way the kid had looked at him. He didn't think it was ridiculous. He thought it was pretty damn close to true. Sarah and her kid, maybe both of them, had gone crazy. "Oh, no. Oh, shit," he said. "We've been courting Henry Ryan for months. You don't think he'd pull out of Baxter Smiley because of this?"

JT looked confused. "Because of what?"

"Because Carol Ryan Memorial Elementary is his shrine to his dead wife. If Erik's kids got chucked out, does that mess up our deal?"

"That's what you're thinking about?" JT said, incredulous. "You are a cold man, my brother."

"It's not cold, JT. It's my partnership."

"It's your partnership at Baxter Smiley. With Lauren Smiley. And Erik Finley." JT glanced at him. "I still don't get why you're working there."

"I know you don't like them," Charlie said.

"*You* don't like them. That's the part I don't understand. You don't like them. You don't need them. What makes you want this so much?"

"Baxter Smiley means something, JT. Lauren isn't exactly the perfect boss, but the firm has been there for a hundred years. If I have Baxter Smiley on my business card, it matters."

JT shrugged. "You're better than them."

"Leave it alone, would you?"

JT dropped it. JT never understood why he wanted the partnership so much. Even though they were brothers, they'd always been different. JT was content to make his own way, be his own man. Charlie wanted to be part of Baxter Smiley because he knew, once he had that partnership, he'd finally be part of a team that meant something. His whole screwy childhood and oddball family would fade to the background once he had a hundred years of Baxter Smiley backing him up. And then maybe he could relax. Once he knew he had that partnership and no one could take it from him…yeah. Maybe then he could relax.

CHARLIE'S CONDOMINIUM WAS in a new building with a view of the river. He'd been one of the early investors, so he'd gotten a choice corner unit on the tenth floor.

It was the first place he'd ever owned, and he'd relished the specificity he'd been able to apply to the details—he'd chosen every appliance, every doorknob, every element of the environmental systems and wiring. But more important, he'd upgraded the soundproofing so even though he had neighbors on one side and below him, he never heard them. On an ordinary night he enjoyed coming home. On a night like this, when he felt he'd lost control in some important ways, he could almost kiss the thick wooden floor.

He changed into jeans and a button-down and rubbed a towel through his hair. His brother was parked in front of the plasma TV watching the Phillies. Charlie threw some pizza in the microwave, cracked a beer, handed another one to his brother, and was just about back to feeling like he could fake normal, even if he wasn't all the way back there yet.

JT's cell rang and Charlie cautioned, "Don't answer it."

JT glared at him. "My wife is about to give birth any second. 'Don't answer it' isn't an option."

Charlie noticed he held the phone gingerly, a few inches from his ear, though.

"I'm on my way," JT said after he'd listened for a few minutes. And then, "Both of us?"

Charlie shook his head emphatically and mouthed the word *No.*

"Charlie doesn't want to get wet again," JT said.

Charlie settled deeper into the black leather couch and took a swig of his beer, but almost spat it back out when he heard his brother say, "All right. He's coming," before he hung up.

"No," Charlie said. "No. He's not." Jimmy Rollins was at bat on TV. *Go, Philly.* He stared at the number eleven on Rollins's back as if he were keeping the man alive with the force of it. He turned the volume up and tossed the remote onto the table.

JT grabbed the remote to turn the volume back down. "Hailey said you have to."

"Hailey's not my mommy." Charlie snatched the remote back from JT and held the volume button while his brother tried to wrestle it away from him. Giving up, JT punched him and then smacked the power button on the front of the TV. The sudden silence was startling. Charlie felt a pit in his stomach—thirty-one years and eleven months of being a younger brother had honed his sense of "You're about to get screwed so you might as well give in now and try to spare your dignity."

"No. She's not your mommy. She's my wife and she's very pregnant. That makes her very scary. She told me to bring you back over there and I'm doing it. If you want to explain to her why you can't stay, feel free. But you will show up."

Charlie crossed his legs on the table. "I'm not going back there, JT. Not today."

JT pulled his cell out and pressed a button. "Hailey?" he said. "Charlie wants to talk to you."

He shoved the phone at Charlie, who tried to push it away, but JT dropped it in his lap. *God,* his brother was such a child. He kicked JT's shin, wishing he had shoes on, and picked the phone up.

"Charlie?" Hailey said. "You better not be about to tell me you're not coming, because if you are—"

Charlie wasn't stupid enough to imagine he could win an argument when Hailey sounded like that. "I'm coming," he said.

"Oh." Her voice had gone back to normal as quickly as flipping a switch. "So what did you want?"

"Just to tell you how happy I am that you married my brother."

He tried not to cringe during the charged silence before she said, "Sarcasm is unattractive." She cut the connection.

If he hadn't been so tired he might have taken a swing at JT to wipe the smirk off his face. He contented himself with snagging the beer out of his brother's hands. When JT protested, Charlie said, "No drinking. You're driving."

He drained his own beer on the way to the kitchen and eyed JT's half-full bottle but reconsidered. He had to get up and into the office early tomorrow. Couldn't afford a hangover.

CHAPTER THREE

"YOU HAVE TO COME," Hailey whispered. The three of them were huddled in a corner of the Finleys' kitchen. Sarah was upstairs changing. "This is the Drunken Breakdown, and in case you haven't noticed, I'm pregnant."

"So?"

"So, I can't get drunk and the Drunken Breakdown doesn't work with sober people."

Charlie looked at JT, but his brother seemed as baffled as he felt. "What are you talking about, Hailey?"

"The Drunken Breakdown. Sarah never did this when she found out Erik had been cheating on her or when he left. She really should have done it when he moved in with Lauren, but that was the night of the silent auction at school and she had to run the raffle. She got behind in the breakdown process. Today the bill came due."

He looked at JT again. His brother shrugged.

"Can you please speak English and not *Cosmo* or Oprah or whatever you're talking now?"

From his position just outside of Hailey's sight line, JT mouthed *"Cosmo?"* and raised an eyebrow. Charlie gave him the finger.

"Erik," Hailey said, "is a bastard, and he screwed

Sarah over. She needs to get that out of her system by having a Drunken Breakdown. That means we go out. We drink too much. We say rude things about Erik. It's cathartic."

"You and JT can take her. He can get drunk and you can say rude things." He didn't add "obviously."

"JT can't get drunk," Hailey said, and Charlie had to admire the way she sounded affronted as if she were making perfect sense and he was the crazy one. "What if I go into labor? He can't be drunk while I'm giving birth—what kind of start in life would that be for a baby?"

She had a point. He didn't like to admit he understood any of what she was talking about, but it had started to make a kind of sick sense. Sarah had been unhinged that afternoon. Maybe she needed to finish the job so she could go back to normal. Still, halfway understanding the crazy talk and actually participating were two different things.

"Call one of her friends."

Hailey shook her head. "Too late. Look, Charlie, as soon as we fed the kids, she took them upstairs and gave them baths. She read to them, talked to them about the day and put them to bed. She did everything right, so when they went to sleep, they didn't have this crappy day hanging over them anymore. Now she needs someone to do that for her. She's had two glasses of wine and I guarantee she won't last through a whole bottle. Come with us and we'll be home by ten-thirty. Eleven at the latest. Olivia's here to babysit. We can tackle this breakdown now and get it over with."

Was this really what chicks did for one another?

Wouldn't it have been better for someone to make her soup and tuck her into bed? That thought brought back memories of Sarah's curls and how soft they'd been when he fixed her headband that afternoon. She'd stood and let him do it as if she were helpless, as if she'd lost the power to care for herself.

What had Hailey said? Sarah pulled herself together for the kids. Even when she'd had her fit at Baxter Smiley she'd made sure to leave them downstairs. So if he did this, if he helped with this twisted support group, maybe that would end it. For her and her kids.

"Fine," he said. "But only if we go someplace where they have the game on. And only if you swear we'll be home by eleven. And no singing."

JT nodded. "Definitely no singing. Especially by you."

Charlie didn't have the energy to give him the finger again.

"Done," Hailey said. "We'll hit Wilton's—no risk of running into people she and Erik know."

SARAH HADN'T BEEN TO Wilton's in years. They used to sneak in here in high school—she distinctly remembered the first time. She'd been in her cheerleading uniform and had ordered a Rob Roy because it was the only drink she knew the name of. At Wilton's, "Can you pay in cash?" was much higher on the list of patron qualifications than "Are you even close to legal?" Wilton's, more a "dive" than a "pub," with all-Phillies-all-the-time decor and the ever-present scent of stale beer, was exactly the kind of place Erik hated most. She took a deep breath, inhaling the atmosphere.

Something inside her loosened, as if she'd let her belt out a notch.

Tonight there were four guys at the bar watching the Phillies game and drinking quarter drafts of Yuengling. The jukebox was on but the grimy mirrors reflected an empty dance floor back at them.

She pulled out the family credit card, the one Erik still paid the bills on, and opened a tab. She sent a pitcher to the guys at the bar, bought another pitcher for herself and the McNultys and a root beer for Hailey. When the bartender asked if she needed anything else, she sent another pitcher to the Phillies fans and lifted her glass when they toasted her. Pitchers of Yuengling wouldn't put much of a dent in Erik's bank balance, but she liked knowing he'd see Wilton's name on the statement.

She and Charlie were halfway through their second pitcher and JT had switched to water when the Phillies went into extra innings. The eleven o'clock news team delayed their broadcast until after the game. She knew Hailey had intended for her to get drunk and it was finally working. She'd started out too keyed up, too distracted thinking about Simon—too deeply pissed off that she'd settled for a husband who'd leave his kids in the lurch—to get drunk and weepy over the loss of said husband or her marriage to the jerk.

However, she'd doggedly downed her fair share of the beer that Hailey kept pouring, and she was beginning to feel it. To feel drunk. She did not, however, feel weepy. Not over Erik.

"I want to make a toast," she said. She waited until they were all looking at her. "To Erik and the Snake in the Grass. May they have many years of knowing they're with exactly the person they deserve the most."

They raised their glasses and toasted. That beer went down so easily she almost didn't notice that she'd emptied her glass. She hadn't been drunk in years. Luckily she didn't know anyone at Wilton's tonight except for Hailey and JT. And Charlie.

Charlie was matching her beer for beer. He'd been… well…not exactly friendly. Not at first. She guessed his brother had made him come. Probably wanted a male buffer between himself and any possible girlfriend talk between her and Hailey. The poor guy was doing his best, but he seemed uncomfortable. She didn't think he'd addressed her directly, not even when the two of them were in the backseat of JT's car on the ride from the house. She didn't blame him. She'd been out of control at Baxter Smiley and he'd had to pick up the pieces.

But he hadn't been rude tonight, just quiet and periodically distracted by the game. Every once in a while she'd catch him watching her too closely, but maybe that was justified.

"Sorry about the office," she blurted. "I didn't mean to break everything."

"It's no big deal." He didn't seem to know what else to say. "Nobody got hurt."

"Only because Erik wasn't there." She'd meant it to sound funny or maybe Angelina Jolie kick-butt scary— *ooh, Sarah wants to kill her cheating ex-husband*—but somehow it came out sounding sad, like she cared about Erik. Like he'd hurt her. Like the weepy part of the evening was going to start. *Typical.*

She'd spent too long caring what people thought of her to achieve defiance easily.

There was an awkward moment when no one was looking at anyone else.

Then Charlie surprised her by clinking his glass against hers. "Hope his boat springs a leak." He squinted, almost as if he were trying to remember something, then added, "Bastard."

That seemed to please him, because he nodded and bumped Hailey with his elbow and said, "That how you do it?"

"Perfect." The way they beamed at each other made Sarah think of a puppy obedience class. Charlie might as well have been wagging his tail. If Hailey'd had a pocketful of biscuits, she'd surely have tossed him one.

JT looked from his brother to his wife. "Hey, I can be insulting, too. Um…hope his passport gets revoked. Bastard."

They all clinked their glasses together.

Charlie went again. "Hope he gets put in one of those tropical jails where they only serve rice and he doesn't get to wear shoes and the radio only gets the polka channel."

JT snorted at that.

Sarah poured another beer, feeling almost cheerful. She wasn't sure if it was the drinks or watching the McNulty brothers get the hang of the Drunken Breakdown. The night was looking up. One of the Phillies must have done something good because the bar erupted in cheers and both men whipped around to check the TV.

"Did I tell you why the kids did it?" Sarah asked Hailey. "Lily thought if there was a really bad problem at school that Erik would have to show up. Can you believe that? It's like every stupid article I ever laughed at in every stupid parenting magazine. If your child is acting out, maybe they need attention. Which is hard to get if their dad is in Bermuda on a boat." She swallowed a mouthful of beer. She could feel her grip on her emotions slipping, her usual public cover dissolving, but for once that was okay. She was supposed to break down tonight. That was the point. "I can't believe I'm putting them through this."

Hailey absently traced the edges of the Phillies logo some patron had carved into the table. "You're not putting them through anything. You can't blame your-self for this."

"Oh, yes, I can," Sarah said. "I married the jerk. My kids are stuck with an…an *ignoramus* as a father because I settled for the booby prize in the husband lottery. I can absolutely blame myself for that. And I do." She nodded emphatically.

Charlie, who hadn't seemed to be listening but must have caught the drift of her comments, lifted his glass and said, "Bastard." They all toasted again and Sarah smiled at the table. The McNultys were really good at this. She eyed the almost empty pitcher. About time for a refill.

"Hey, JT," Hailey said. "We should dance. Lord knows we won't be getting out again anytime soon."

JT craned his neck to see the dance floor. "I'm not sure people actually dance at Wilton's. I think they have that space more for brawls or, you know, passing out while you wait for your ride to do one more shot."

"Nice try, buddy," Sarah said. She propped an elbow on the table, sipped her beer and waited for Hailey to set him straight.

"Get up," Hailey said.

"Yes, ma'am. I do love dancing." He gave one last glance at the TV. "Keep an eye on the bull pen," he told Charlie before grabbing Hailey's hand and heading toward the back.

She couldn't tell if Charlie was drunk or tired or what, but his usual poise slipped and she was able to watch as he struggled to decide what to do. He tracked JT and Hailey as they crossed the bar and then he looked longingly at the door, before sighing loudly and lifting his beer. Their eyes met as he put his glass down, and his ears blushed red when he realized how transparent he'd been. She supposed she should be insulted, but he was too adorable. Besides, she owed him.

"It's okay, Charlie. We don't have to dance," she said, even as she liked him a little better for knowing he was supposed to ask. "This is no fun for you. Why don't you go?"

He snorted. "I'm being a jerk, that's why. Sorry." He drained his beer and set the glass on the table. "Want me to say more rude things about Erik? Because I have a whole bunch saved up."

She smiled at that but shook her head.

"Would you rather dance? It's your Drunken Breakdown, you make the call."

She shook her head again, but then stopped because

it was possible she'd had too much beer to shake her head safely. "You've done more than enough."

He looked as if he might protest, but she went on, "I'm serious. I'm thirty-four, right? I know there's no such thing as knights in shining armor. Which is okay. It's okay." She put her hand on his arm, patting him. Reassuring them both that she was, in fact, okay. "But you, Charlie. You know what you do? You step up." She was still patting him and she really should stop, but his arm was delightfully firm and she was enjoying herself. "Doesn't matter what's going on, you figure out what needs to be done and then you do that. You don't even want to be here but that doesn't matter."

"I drank some beer, watched the game and said rude things about Erik," he said. "It's not like I'm not enjoying myself."

"You weren't enjoying yourself this afternoon when you had to catch that vase I threw at the secretary."

His eyes flickered away, like a tiny flinch. He probably wished she hadn't brought that up. "You missed Madison by a mile."

"You're being nice again."

"So, how about a dance, then?"

She rested her hand on his arm. He was so solid. He'd calmed her down and gotten her home this afternoon. Now he was here and he knew she wanted to dance, and he was asking because he should, even though the Phillies were in extra innings and she was sure it was past time for him to be home.

He wasn't a knight in shining armor, but this gift he had for doing the right thing at the right time was so appealing—she'd felt out of step her whole life. Maybe for this night, she'd lean on him. Be with someone who was in step, maybe be in step herself.

Plus, honestly? Charlie was tall and his eyes were kind, and earlier when they'd first come in, his hair had been damp and she'd wanted, for one tiny second, to comb her fingers through it. And he'd just asked her if she wanted to dance. She loved to dance.

"Dance," she said. "Yes, please."

He surprised her by turning his arm over and sliding it until his hand rested under hers. His hand was big and warm, and when his fingers closed on hers, the strength in them surprised her.

"When Erik holds my hand it's just like holding a hamburger bun," she said. She squeezed his. Firm. Not one bit squishy.

The corner of Charlie's mouth quirked up and he squeezed her hand back. "I'm not Erik, Sarah."

No. He definitely wasn't Erik. She'd known Charlie practically her entire life, JT's little brother, the quarterback on their high school football team, and then Erik's colleague at work.

So why had she never noticed that his blue eyes were so dark they were almost navy, or that his dark eyelashes were so long and thick she knew a hundred women who'd kill for them?

God, I must be drunk. But not too drunk to appreciate a hot guy.

She'd known he was good-looking. It was hard to miss with his broad shoulders and the varsity-athlete swagger he'd never lost, which made his walk so unconsciously sexy. But as Sarah followed him toward the dance floor at the back of Wilton's, her hand felt warmer than it should in his grasp and she couldn't stop looking at the way his jeans fit his ass just right.

"I like your jeans," she said, admiring the way the dark denim of his 7 brand jeans accentuated the long, lean length of his thighs. "Erik still wears high-rise Levi's, same ones he's been buying since 1989." She reached out and touched his belt where it rested low and sexy on his hip. "His belt loops are up around his armpits."

Charlie laughed, pulling her hand in against the small of his back. "I realize this whole breakdown is about Erik," he said. "But could we stop talking about him? I'm pissed enough without hearing about his pants."

"Right," she agreed. "Okay. No more Erik." Charlie was wise. And he was here, right here with her. She touched his hip again. It was past time she was finished with Erik. Time for her to move on to plan B and for right now, in this bar tonight plan B was looking an awful lot like a dance with Charlie McNulty.

The dance floor was empty except for Hailey and JT. JT was holding Hailey carefully and she had her arms locked around his neck as they swayed in place to "Moon River."

"Andy Williams?" Charlie called.

"The jukebox is limited," JT said. "Besides, it was Hailey's dollar."

"You can't tell me you don't like this song," Hailey said. "*Breakfast at Tiffany's*? Start dancing."

"Is that what you're doing? Dancing?" Charlie asked.

"Oh, God. It's Wilton's, Charlie. Nobody's keeping score." JT groaned and buried his face in Hailey's neck. "Don't look, wife. He's doing it again."

Charlie turned his back on his brother and, with a challenge in his eye, asked, "You like to dance, Sarah?"

"Um, yeah. I do." She wasn't sure what JT had been talking about with the whole "cover your eyes thing." Maybe Charlie was a terrible dancer. She put one hand on his shoulder and the other at his waist and expected him to start shifting from foot to foot and shuffling in a halfhearted circle like JT, in fact, like every guy she'd ever danced with.

But when he settled a hand on her waist and squeezed her other hand, she felt it, the pure confidence of a guy who knew his way around the dance floor. Her pulse kicked up and she settled herself into the rhythm as he spun them onto the wooden floor. The man really knew how to lead, and she found it freed her to enjoy the dance in a way that nothing else did.

Sarah was a good dancer. Turned out Charlie McNulty was, too. She didn't feel drunk once they started dancing, just loose and free, and very much in tune with him.

Each time he spun her out, she knew exactly how to come back so that she fit into his waiting hands in perfect time. Each time he slid his foot forward or pressed her hip to change direction, she was ready to move with him. She loved the strength in his arms and the firm, coiled balance in his chest and waist. He held her and she felt in step, perfectly in synch with the world for once in her life.

But most of all, she loved his sense of fun. She caught him watching JT and Hailey, and when his brother looked over, he spun her forward and then back under his arm and slid their linked hands low across his stomach. She understood then that they were putting on a show for JT, and she shimmied smooth and easy as she passed behind Charlie. Even though she knew it was all part of the dance, the heat coming off his body stirred nerves she thought Erik had put to sleep forever. When she faced him again for a three-quarter turn, her skin was flushed—she hoped he'd think it was exertion. Her pulse didn't settle down again until the song was over.

They finished with a show-offy dip and she laughed when JT gave Charlie the finger. "Just because my partner's pregnant is no reason to put on a dance expo," he said. "You're making Hailey feel inadequate."

"There was only one inadequate person out here and it sure wasn't the pregnant lady."

Sarah liked listening to them tweak each other. She liked that Charlie was still holding her hand even more.

Hailey patted JT's shoulder. "Don't let him bother you. At least you're still taller."

"Hey," Charlie protested.

Hailey stopped next to the jukebox and dropped a quarter in. She punched in a number and waved to them. "Have fun, kiddies!"

When the next song started, it was "Jump, Jive an' Wail." Charlie raised an eyebrow and she shook her head. This was Wilton's. He wouldn't want to…but he did. The two of them did put on a dance expo then. Not that anyone else in Wilton's noticed. But Sarah threw herself into the music, and when Charlie met her spin for spin and kick for kick, it just made her go harder and higher than before. She had forgotten that she really, really loved to dance. How did a woman forget something like that? Oh, yeah. *Erik.*

When the song ended, they made their way back to the table. Hailey slid off her stool and asked JT to walk with her to the bathroom.

Sarah picked up Hailey's water glass and took a gulp. It didn't do much to cool her down. Possibly because Charlie was standing next to her, one foot on the bottom rung of her stool, his arm across the wooden back, fingertips lightly brushing her shoulder.

"Where'd you learn to dance?" he asked.

"Pageants. My mom had me in them starting with those Beautiful Baby things they do at the mall. Dance was my talent."

"I guess so," Charlie said. His voice was deep, and she liked hearing it rumble up from his chest so close to her ear.

"Drove my mom crazy that I never won. My dancing was good, but "bubbly" is always going to be the runner-up to gorgeous, long-legged and, you know, endowed."

He smiled. "Doesn't seem fair if they took points off for being short."

She was glad he hadn't tried to reassure her about her looks. Doing pageants for all those years had given her clarity about herself. She'd learned how to work harder and engage more with people so she was a consistent top finisher, but all the smiling in the world was not going to make her beautiful. "What about you? Judging by JT's performance, you didn't learn to dance from your parents."

"An old girlfriend made me take lessons. I think she was priming me for an engagement. She probably imagined we were practicing for the wedding dance."

"What happened to the girlfriend?"

"I liked dancing more than I liked her, I guess."

When they'd been dancing, it had become even more apparent that Charlie had very nice shoulders. She wondered what it would feel like if she rested her head on his shoulder while they finished this interesting conversation, but the whole drunken part of the night was catching up to her. She was tired and Charlie smelled wonderful, and if she could put her head on his shoulder just until Hailey and JT came back then maybe she could face tomorrow again.

Her head was halfway to his shoulder when she stopped herself. He'd been nothing but kind. That was all it was. His brother and sister-in-law had convinced him to be here and she shouldn't take advantage.

"You ever wonder about it? Getting married?" She rubbed her finger in the wet circle Hailey's glass had left on the table. "I'm surprised that girl let you get away. You have a lot of very nice qualities."

He gave her a half smile, his eyes crinkling at the corners. "Nice qualities, huh?" he said before adding, "I used to know exactly how I felt about getting married. No thanks. Melanie and Jack McNulty's *epic love* wasn't so epic when you had to live in the same house with it."

He paused, and she saw him meet his brother's eyes

as he came back with Hailey. "Those two, though, they're enough to make anybody reconsider the subject."

"People having a Drunken Breakdown because of a two-timing spouse really shouldn't consider marriage in a positive light no matter what, but I'm with you on that one. Too bad everybody doesn't get what JT and Hailey have."

"Erik's an idiot," Charlie said quietly. She almost cried then. But he didn't deserve that.

"Hope his boat springs a leak," she answered.

"Bastard," they said together.

"Thanks, Charlie," she said. "For taking care of me. And drinking beer with me and going dancing with me. You…you're not…this is going to come out wrong, but I've had too much beer to figure out how to say it better. You're nicer than I realized. I had a crappy day, but this has been a decent night."

He tucked his chin in, as if he was surprised. Or hurt. She hoped he wasn't hurt. She'd meant to compliment him. But then he gave her a quick kiss on the cheek, leaning his forehead on her hair for an instant while he murmured, "You're all right, too, Sarah."

Back in JT's car, she rested her head on the seat and closed her eyes. She didn't want to talk to anyone. The night had turned out much better than she could have imagined. She didn't want to ruin it with reality.

JT PULLED UP OUTSIDE Sarah's house and Charlie felt bad about waking her up. She looked peaceful, sunk into the seat with her eyes closed. Her headband had slipped forward again, but he didn't touch it. He'd had a little too much fun touching Sarah on the dance floor and he really didn't need any more temptation. He couldn't believe he'd let loose like that in Wilton's of all places. He liked to dance, sure, but he didn't usually do it in the middle of a bar. He'd felt bad that she saw him thinking about escaping, and he'd started out trying to make it up to her. By the time they finished, he'd been, well, if he was doing anybody a favor there when he'd had his hands on Sarah's body as they danced, it had been himself.

"Sarah," he called softly. "You're home."

She didn't stir. He tapped Hailey's shoulder. "Your friend is asleep back here, Hailey. You need to help her up."

Hailey's eyes opened wide and she crossed her arms. "I'm eight thousand months pregnant, Charlie. I'm not getting out of this car unless it's to go to the hospital or my bed. Take her in the house and tell Olivia we're waiting."

He was going to be so happy when she finally had the baby and he had his normal sister-in-law back. He got out and went around to Sarah's door. When the cooler night air hit her, her eyes drifted open. "We're here," he said.

She pulled herself up and climbed out. He walked next to her up the stairs. She opened the front door and he stepped in behind her to wait for Olivia.

There was a scarf on the floor and he picked it up and handed it to her. She looked startled and then wadded it up in her hand. "I dropped that when I was changing before I picked up Simon. I was worried I'd look frivolous if I wore it. Stupid, huh?"

"It's not stupid to care about what people think. You were trying to help your kids."

"I guess."

She was still holding the scarf and looking lost, and even though he had a strict rule about getting involved in other people's problems, he figured he owed her something—this was supposed to have been her Drunken Breakdown, after all, and as far as he could tell she hadn't done much breaking down. Not after the office, anyway.

"You okay?"

The afternoon must have been on her mind, too. "By 'okay' do you mean am I finished pitching fits?"

"I guess that's part of the question."

"I'm not sure." She stuffed the scarf in the pocket of her jeans and then pushed her headband back into place. She didn't look drunk at all then and certainly not crazy. "I'm not sure I'm finished yet. Today was horrible, but trashing the office felt good. I'm glad Erik will finally know how I feel."

He hadn't expected that answer. Sarah Finley had always been pretty much the definition of normal. How could someone like her skid so far off the rails in one day? He guessed he shouldn't really be asking that question since it hadn't been an hour since he'd been swing dancing with his boss's ex-wife at Wilton's.

"I hope you get in touch with him," Charlie said. "He's going to be concerned about this and not just because of the kids."

"What do you mean?"

"We've been trying to get the Ryan family account for months now. Henry Ryan lives and breathes his wife's memory, which is all wrapped up in that school."

Sarah's mouth tightened. "I hardly think Henry Ryan's money should be the most pressing concern for Erik or my children," she said. He opened his mouth to explain, but she pushed on. "Or anyone."

She brushed past him and disappeared into the house calling for Olivia. He waited, but when his niece appeared, Sarah wasn't with her. Charlie didn't have a chance to say goodbye or to tell her that he hadn't meant anything except what he'd said. The Ryan account was important to Baxter Smiley, and Erik was going to need to consider that while they did whatever they needed to do for the kids. It was all well and good to mess around at Wilton's, but the world was still out there and nothing had changed.

Including him. He might have gone to his first Drunken Breakdown and done some dancing in the back of Wilton's bar. He might even have kissed Sarah. He didn't know why he'd done that. He certainly hadn't meant to kiss Erik's wife. Ex-wife. But the way she'd looked at him as if they'd made a connection, as if she *saw* him, well, he hadn't been able to ignore it. Good thing it had only been a peck on the cheek. Because tomorrow when he woke up, he needed to put this all behind him and get the Ryan deal back on track.

CHAPTER FOUR

SARAH GOT UP AT HER regular time the next morning. She made herself a plate of scrambled eggs and toast and took it out on the patio to eat, sinking into the thick striped cushion on a teak love seat. She'd grown up in this house and had always loved it. When her parents had offered it to her and Erik as a wedding present before they moved to Florida, she'd been delighted and Erik had been over the moon. Statlerville was a status-conscious place, and this sprawling turn-of-the-century house with its dark woodwork, plaster walls and narrow back servants' staircase was smack in the middle of the neighborhood with high-status addresses. Houses didn't come up for sale here often, and when they did, it was usually a private sale.

Sarah had wondered more than once in the past few years if Erik had married her mostly for a shot at the house. Which had been depressing enough in a very Regency-heroine-sold-for-the-dowry kind of way even before he'd traded up for Lauren Smiley, presumably getting a woman he liked better in addition to a better address.

Not that she minded him leaving all that much. She'd gotten tired of Erik's frequent absences and constant criticism long before he'd actually told her he was moving out.

What she minded was that she was now divorced. She didn't miss Erik, but being married had been comforting. She'd fit right in with the other women in this neighborhood with their overindulged children, schedules full of charity work and a tasteful piece of jewelry from their husbands at Christmas. For the first time in her life, Sarah had felt as if she'd won. She'd worked hard, kept Eric happy, coped with the house and the kids, and it still hadn't been enough.

Now she was divorced and nobody quite knew what to do with her. She was mortified that all of her friends knew Erik had cheated on her and had left her for the Snake. People she and Erik had socialized with from Baxter Smiley avoided her. Even some of their non-work-related friends had stopped calling. So for everything she'd done to fit in and be part of things, she wasn't quite normal. She was just glad her parents had died a few years ago—her mom would have been devastated.

Beyond the disruption in her life, she couldn't believe that she'd let Erik remodel the kitchen right before he split. He'd used a contractor Lauren had recommended—and that he'd let that woman's opinion into her home made Sarah's blood boil. Erik and the contractor had gone with an all-bigger, all-the-time concept. The roof had been raised, beams added, walls pushed back, and the result was a showplace Sarah didn't feel comfortable in. How could she when she had to use a stool to reach all but the bottom two shelves in the cupboards? He'd even installed a custom-built chandelier over the table that was roped with silver medallions, each one engraved with their monogram—EFS. He'd said the medallions were a modern take on the old-fashioned crystal motif. She'd thought they were tacky no matter the motif.

It was twisted that the remodel bothered her almost as much as the divorce, but these past few years she'd spent a lot more time with the kitchen than she had with Erik. With the exception of the kitchen, she liked the house a whole lot better than him, too.

She'd taken to spending as much time as she could on the patio, where she enjoyed the peace. The canvas awning covered two-thirds of the length, keeping that section cool. The outdoor fireplace made for cozy evenings. It had been nicer when Hailey and Olivia lived in the carriage house just across the driveway and she ran into them all the time. But even now with the carriage house empty after Hailey and JT bought their house, the patio remained her favorite place.

The French door to the kitchen opened and Lily emerged. She was freshly showered and dressed in a pair of pink capris with a white T-shirt. Her shoulder-length hair, blond like Sarah's, but straight—a genetic mystery since Sarah and her mom both had curly hair and Erik's was wavy, too—had been neatly combed, every hair in exactly the right place as only a true perfectionist could accomplish. Sarah sometimes thought Lily willed her hair straight because curls were too messy.

"Are we allowed to do our work even if we're not allowed to be at school, or is getting behind part of the punishment?"

Sarah smiled at her daughter and held out her arm. Lily climbed onto the cushioned love seat next to her but didn't snuggle the way Simon would have. "Honey, they don't punish kids by making them get behind in their work. But wouldn't you like a vacation? We could drive out to Dorney Park and spend the day."

"Cool," Simon said.

Sarah hadn't heard him come out. She was surprised to see him, actually. He'd been a night owl ever since his infancy when his night-long crying jags had sent Erik to sleep in the guest room for the first time. Everyone had told Sarah she needed to teach the baby to sleep, and she'd actually tried the systems her friends swore by, but her efforts had only made Simon furious and broken her heart. She'd ended up bringing him into bed with her, where she would doze while he babbled and nursed most of the night.

Nowadays he was closer to a daytime schedule because he had to be up for school, but on days off he rarely emerged downstairs before nine or ten.

"Hi, sweetie," Sarah said. He sat on her other side, his hair sticking up and his pajama top on backward.

"I missed a test yesterday already," Lily said. "And if I don't get my homework I'll get zeros and I was the only one in the class who didn't have a zero all year. I also had perfect attendance, but I don't have that anymore, either." She wasn't whining, Lily didn't whine. But she was definitely implying that Sarah was slightly thick and thank goodness she had a daughter like Lily to keep her on the straight and narrow.

Sarah was heartily sick of the straight and narrow. Sick of feeling like a loser every time she detoured off the path.

That was why she replied more sharply than she would have normally. "I'll see if I can get your work. But maybe we need to have a chat about exactly why you're not in school this week."

Simon flung an arm around her waist, but Lily stiffened.

"You said you weren't mad," she said.

"I'm not mad. Not mad, but I have questions. We have to talk about it."

Lily crossed her arms. Sarah touched her shoulder. "Why did you give Simon the knife? Can you tell me what you were thinking?"

She'd decided it would be better if Lily brought Erik up first. But her daughter's answer surprised her.

"I was going to take the knife. He made me let him help. He said if I took it in no one would believe I was going to hurt anyone."

"No one would believe…what?"

"He was right. If I brought it in, Mrs. Camp would have thought it was a mistake or something. No one would think I was trying to…you know."

"Attack your classmates?"

"Right."

"But they would believe it about Simon?"

Lily shrugged. "He's Simon. Duh."

Sarah glanced down. Her son's eyes were tightly shut. She knew from her own childhood that wasn't an effective way to not hear what people were saying about you. That one devastating *duh* from Lily summed up so much of her own worries for Simon. He was six and he was already in the "duh, of course he's a weirdo" category? How had that happened?

"Lily, you have your differences with your brother, but the idea that you brought him into your plan and got him in trouble is very upsetting. He's too little to know better."

"I did so know better," Simon said.

Simon apparently was also too little to recognize a bone when one was thrown his way.

"He wanted to help," Lily said.

Simon added, "I *wanted* Dad to come because Lily wanted to see him. Lily said he would come but he didn't. Which means this was a bad plan." He poked Lily. "Next time we're doing my plan."

"Your plan was stupid."

"It was not stupid."

"It was. First of all, you don't even know any hackers. And Carson doesn't count—he *guessed* your Webkinz password, he didn't hack it."

"Guessing is like hacking. If we guessed Dad's password and crashed his work computer he'd have come home."

"Stop," Sarah said. "First of all, Dad would have come to school with me, but there wasn't time for him to get there from Bermuda. It's far away." She was pretty sure that was true. Erik would have come with her. He might have fallen into the habit of ignoring the kids, but he'd still be there for the big stuff. "And second, why did you want to see Dad?"

"I don't… I mean…he missed the tryouts for baseball," Lily muttered. "He never missed tryouts before and now we're almost ready to start games and he's still gone."

That was the first thing about this situation that made

any sense. Her children had spent three weeks planning this…caper…because they couldn't figure out a better way to get Erik's attention. It hadn't registered at the time, but he should have been at Lily's baseball tryouts. He was the one who'd pushed her into sports—his insanity about achievement had met its perfect match in Lily's intense perfectionism and natural talent for athletics. Lily was naturally talented at just about everything, but baseball was her game. She played catcher with a ferocity that intimidated opponents and sometimes overwhelmed her own pitchers. She and Erik had always connected over her baseball career, but this year he'd been kept busy shacking up with the Boss.

He was supposed to have the kids every other weekend but he'd missed a few visits in a row before he and Lauren left on their jaunt. He had taken them for dinner a few times, but those were quick—pick them up when he got home from work at six-thirty and then back home for bedtime at eight.

How long had it been since they'd spent any real time with him? She felt guilty that she hadn't pushed it with him. She liked having the kids to herself, and even while he was breaking the agreement they'd made, it hadn't bothered her. She should have noticed that it was bothering the kids. She was going to need to pay much better attention to this. No matter how much she loathed asking him for anything.

"Okay. Here's the thing," Sarah said. "I wish you'd told me how much you're missing Dad. I could have helped with that. Your dad loves you. He wouldn't want you to feel this way."

He might hope that they didn't miss him so he could travel the world for weeks at a time, but he wouldn't leave them hanging. Except that he had. She hoped this was a blip and not a trend. He'd been really good about showing up for the scheduled visits in the beginning. Maybe he'd been too focused on this trip with Lauren. She had a bad feeling in her stomach, though. Erik was spoiled and selfish. She hoped he wouldn't become the dad who felt his kids were an inconvenience.

"So I'm going to call him and find out when he's coming and I'll tell you guys what I find out."

Lily nodded exactly as if she were taking mental notes and had just labeled a sheet "Mom's Plan to Fix the Family" and written down point A. If only Sarah had any clue of how to fix the family. Getting Erik to show up would be a first step.

"Next, I'll call the school and get your work. I'll try to help you keep up while you're home."

"Will you ask about the zeros?"

She swallowed a sigh and nodded. The last thing Sarah wanted to do was ask anyone at that school for anything even close to resembling a favor, but for Lily she would do it.

"Third, we're going to Dorney Park today. We all need to blow off some steam, and getting whipped around on the Scrambler sounds like the perfect plan." She didn't add that she needed to reassure herself that her nine-year-old daughter remembered how to have fun.

Simon's smile was just as pure and sweet as it had always been. Clenching her teeth, she thought, *Fourth,*

I'm going to figure out why Simon is already on the outside looking in.

"Will you guys go in and get some cereal? Simon, take a shower when you're finished. I'll come up and turn the water on for you."

Simon said okay, but then waited for Lily to go back inside before he said, "*I* don't miss Dad. I did the plan because Lily misses him. So when you talk to him, you don't have to say I miss him, because I don't."

"You don't?"

"We don't do things together the way he does with Lily. Besides, I love you best."

Sarah put her hands on his shoulders. "This is tough, buddy, but it's okay to miss him."

Simon scratched one bare foot against the back of his calf. "It's okay not to miss him, too, right?"

There wasn't an answer for that. She pulled him close for a hug. "It's okay for you to feel whatever you feel, Simon. Always okay."

After they went inside, she pulled her phone out and scrolled to the number Charlie had given her yesterday. Erik's cell phone had been going straight to voice mail since shortly after he left. She didn't know if he'd lost it or stopped answering on purpose. She hadn't minded until yesterday when she'd needed to get in touch with him and couldn't, and she realized how stupid it was that she didn't have a contact number for the children's father.

But now she did. "Erik on Yacht" was right there in her contacts list, perfectly alphabetized between Ellie Martin and First Street, her favorite pizza place, proving that the scene at Baxter Smiley had not been, as she'd hoped, a bad dream. The number was there, which meant she'd actually typed it into her phone in front of Kimberly Sills in the lobby restroom while Charlie handed her a bunch of paper towels.

Charlie had really come through for her. She knew he was an extremely buttoned-down person, but he'd taken her into the ladies' room to help her get herself together away from her kids. Of all the nice things people had done for her in her life, that was probably both the most bizarre and one of the most thoughtful.

She looked at the number again but then snapped the phone shut. She needed to plan a little bit more. It was as if she'd been sleepwalking, fooling herself that if she didn't look at her life too closely, she wouldn't have to see that everything was wrong.

Erik had said as much to her. When he'd told her he was moving in with Lauren, she'd begged him to reconsider, for the kids' sake, to try therapy with her. Something. To try to save what they had. He'd laughed. "What we have?"

Sarah remembered the sick feeling in her stomach—she'd thought it was sadness, but now she wondered if it hadn't been the truth settling in. "We don't have anything worth saving," he'd said. "This marriage has been over for years. You just didn't have the guts to leave first."

Guts. As if leaving a marriage, a family, a promise, was something to be proud of. No, she'd never had that kind of guts. Never wanted to. But she also hadn't had the kind of courage required to see her life for what it really was.

She'd spent her childhood as the runner-up, and not

just in the pageants her mother had insisted on dragging her to. She'd always been second place—from her straight-B report cards to her standing as Hailey's sidekick, to the fact that she knew her parents had spent a lot of money on fertility treatments hoping they could finally "get their boy."

She'd gotten used to working extra hard to be what other people wanted so they wouldn't notice when she came up short. At the same time she developed a thick mask to disguise her unhappiness from herself.

One reason she'd accepted Erik's proposal even though he was far from head over heels in love with her was that she hadn't thought it was possible to find someone who would be head over heels for her. Erik had been, well, willing. He'd also been on the rebound, because he'd proposed to one of her sorority sisters six months earlier and been turned down. She'd never asked, because she couldn't face knowing, but she wondered if he'd even bought her a new ring.

She should have asked. Somewhere deep in an uncomfortable part of her heart, she knew that even if she had asked and even if he'd said it wasn't a new ring, there was a big chance she'd have married him anyway. She wouldn't have thought to ask for more than what he was offering.

But that was her—her life, her mistakes. Erik had divorced her, but what was he going to do about their kids? Charlie had mentioned the Ryan deal and she had no doubt Erik would bring that up when she told him what had happened. He'd be furious that not only had the kids gotten in trouble, but they'd gotten in trouble in a way that would call the wrong kind of attention to their family right before Henry Ryan and his sons signed with Baxter Smiley.

Talking to Lily had opened her eyes. Simon wasn't just *a* suspect. In the eyes of Carol Ryan Memorial Elementary, Simon *was* suspect. He didn't fit in. Would Erik make that worse? Was Simon right in thinking his own father didn't enjoy spending time with him?

No way.

Simon had barely started figuring out who he was. Sarah was damned if she'd let the Carol Ryan Memorial Elementary school or Erik or anyone else tell him he wasn't good enough.

Simon wasn't going to live and breathe "Not Good Enough" his whole childhood the way she had. Following in Lily's wake would be challenging. She gave her daughter credit—Lily had great natural gifts, but she also worked like a dog to get every last ounce she could out of herself. The result was a nine-year-old child with a fairly intimidating résumé. A tough act to follow. So she had to figure out how to explain the situation to Erik in a way that left any concerns about Simon under the rug where his dad wouldn't be able to find them.

CHARLIE STOPPED IN FRONT of Donny's security desk the next morning. "Brought you a present," he said, putting a brown bag containing the bottle of Scotch in front of the guard. Donny didn't touch the bag, but he inclined his head slightly, wrinkling his twice-broken ex-boxer's nose, as if he could smell the Macallan single malt through the paper.

"Not my birthday," Donny said.

"I appreciate your good work."

Charlie didn't smile, disarmingly or otherwise, but Donny did. "You're hoping I won't tell Erik Finley his wife went off the reservation and I had to babysit his kids while she did it?"

Bingo.

"I'm hoping you'll enjoy this fine Scotch."

"Gotcha," Donny said. As Charlie hurried to get the elevator, he heard the security guard mutter, "Erik Finley gave me a two-dollar scratch ticket as my holiday tip last year."

"Bastard," Charlie added under his breath with a smile. That breakdown thing last night had been screwed-up. Confirmed again that he was never going to get what women needed. He'd have thought Sarah would want to stay home and drink tea or watch old movie musicals if she was upset. Who knew draft beer, bad jukebox swing and a couple of insults about her ex would make her feel better?

Just as he was closing the inner door, he heard a woman call, "Hold the elevator."

He opened the door again but wished he hadn't when Kimberly rushed in. She said, "Thanks," but then saw it was him and said, "Oh." He closed the door quickly and pressed the button for her floor.

Kimberly glanced at the lit display of floor numbers and then went for the jugular. She was getting off at three, no time to waste. "When you were in the bathroom with Sarah Finley yesterday, was that before or after she trashed your office?"

The pulse in Charlie's neck seemed to beat loud enough that he could hear it. "I'm sorry we disturbed you," he said.

"Disturbed me? Not at all. It was like watching a car accident, you know, when you can't look away? I told Felix the story last night at dinner. He couldn't believe it. Are you guys pressing charges?"

"What? No." He didn't think they were. Who'd press them? Lauren?

"I heard her kids got thrown out of school, too. Amazing." Kimberly stepped forward as the bell chimed for her floor. "You think you know people." She stepped out. "See you, Charlie."

He closed the inner elevator gate and pushed the button for his floor and then settled back to wait. When he'd been a sophomore in high school, his mom had had an affair with the art teacher from his school. She'd rented a storefront on Main Street and held an exhibition of her paintings while she was taking lessons from the guy. The paintings were all nudes. All her.

His dad had thrown a chair through the window of the exhibit space and so the show ended before it really got started. But enough people had seen the paintings that Charlie had spent the next two weeks at school fighting with just about every dickhead who could make up a dirty joke about a naked woman. That was the only time he'd ever come close to getting suspended, and he'd always thought the school let it go because they didn't want to drag the details out.

He'd felt this same helpless anger then that he felt now about Erik and Lauren and what they were doing to Baxter Smiley. He'd fought those boys back then to shut them up about his mom, but the whole time, all he could think was it was her fault. She'd put herself out there, asked for it. If she'd had the sense to have her stupid affair behind closed doors like a normal person, no one would have known.

Same with Erik. Same with…same with everyone who was stupid enough to drag their problems out and dump them in front of other people. He felt bad for Sarah, no doubt about it, but she should have known better.

As the elevator slowed approaching the fifth floor, he kept his gaze on the ceiling. The doors opened and he stepped out, staring at a point high on the wall over the reception desk. He kept looking up until he'd taken two steps into the lobby and heard and felt only the ordinary, muffled tread of his loafers on the thick wool carpet. No broken pottery crunching underfoot.

"Is there something on the ceiling, Mr. McNulty?" Madison asked.

"No. Everything's fine," he answered as he allowed himself to glance around the lobby. He'd been nervous that the wreckage from yesterday would still be here but the place gleamed with its usual polish. Someone had even ordered fresh flower arrangements to fill the otherwise empty display shelves, leaving no evidence of Sarah's fit. Baxter Smiley was back to normal. Charlie's shoulders relaxed.

When he was a kid and his parents had had one of their throw-the-dishes battles, they'd often left it to him and JT to either clean up themselves or try to figure out a way to live with it until his mom and dad came back to their senses. They always did eventually—Melanie and Jack making up was as upsettingly gross as the screaming matches were frightening—but he was glad he didn't have to deal with the aftermath of yesterday. Baxter Smiley understood appearances.

With the evidence cleared away, he could remember Sarah dancing instead of throwing bookends. Not that he was remembering Sarah. Or wanted to remember Sarah. It was just… Oh, screw it. He hoped she was putting herself back together the way Baxter Smiley had been put back together so everything could continue on as usual. Including him.

Madison was watching him with a nervous look in her eye. "Mr. McNulty?"

"Yes, Madison?"

"Ms. Smiley and Mr. Finley want to speak with you. They're on hold on line three." She tapped the button on her phone that was glowing an ominous orange.

Perfect. Because that was exactly the conversation he'd have picked to start off his day.

"We need you to talk to Henry Ryan," Erik said.

"But don't tell him what you want to talk about," Lauren added.

Charlie waited. He had no idea what they had heard about what happened yesterday. He wasn't about to volunteer details, especially not the part where he danced with and then kissed Erik's ex-wife. He was pretty sure the other man wouldn't understand the Drunken Breakdown ritual.

Lauren and Erik still hadn't said anything. There was

a soft murmuring from their end of the phone. Maybe they were strategizing, but he had a very bad feeling they were kissing each other and the speakerphone was somewhere between them. He hated speakerphones.

"What do I want to talk to him about?" he finally asked.

"The fiasco that happened at the school," Lauren snapped. "But don't bring it up to him first."

"Let me see if I understand," Charlie asked. "I should call him and find out if he knows that Erik's children are in trouble at school, but if he doesn't I shouldn't tell him?"

"Exactly," Lauren said.

"Should I tell him you want to meet him at the Sadie Hawkins dance, too?"

"What?"

"Come on, Lauren, you're better than this. I'm not some middle-school cheerleader trying to drum up a date for her best friend. This is business. I'm not sneaking around."

"You're not telling him about my kids if he doesn't already know," Erik said.

"Maybe he won't care. Don't kids get in trouble at school?" Charlie had gotten in trouble at school. That time when he'd been fighting because of his mom's art show and a few more times over the years. Not as often as JT was in trouble, and it had almost always been his brother's fault, but it still happened.

"Not my kids," Erik said.

"Not his wife's school," Lauren added. "We need to shut this down because we need that account."

Charlie's hand twitched toward the phone base. If

only he could hang up on them. "Why would I be calling about this? They're not my kids."

"You're the one he likes. If we get him, he's your account," Erik said. "And you're on the board at the school, so you have a reason to talk about it."

"But only if he brings it up," Lauren finished.

"The board isn't involved in discipline."

"Get involved," Erik said. "Damn it, Charlie, take care of the situation. This is what it means to be a partner in the firm."

"Fine," Charlie said. It wasn't fine. Not by any stretch. Erik needed to take care of this. It was his family. Charlie didn't want any part of it. The point of being a partner at Baxter Smiley was that messes didn't happen there. How could Lauren not see that she was endangering the reputation for discretion that made Baxter Smiley impressive?

On the other hand, he would rather that the lovebirds stay away from Henry Ryan. He wouldn't put it past either of them to try to steal the old man out from under him. And that old man was his ticket to a position at the top of the firm. A partnership. He'd finally be secure once he got that. He needed the Ryan family to sign on with him.

"When are you coming back, anyway?"

"When our honeymoon is over." Lauren giggled.

"Your honey what?"

"We got married. The divorce came through yesterday and we got married last night. It's a dream come true."

Bastard had never been more fitting. Erik had been getting married while Sarah and his kids were falling apart.

"Aren't you going to congratulate us?" Lauren said.

An image of Sarah toasting at Wilton's came into his head. "I'm glad you both found the person who's exactly right for you," he said.

After more giggling on Lauren's part and an inappropriate, off-color and, in Charlie's opinion, physically improbable boast from Erik, they hung up. How had Sarah put up with that guy for so long?

Charlie placed the phone on the base and stared at the leather portfolio containing his Ryan family game plan.

How was Sarah was going to react to the news of Erik's marriage? He stood up but then sat back down. The less he knew about Sarah and her kids the easier it would be to talk to Henry without complications.

He opened the portfolio to look at the timeline he'd made for securing the Ryan account. He'd been so sure that the proper planning and diligence would bring the appropriate results. Now he was facing this tangle of who knew what emotions and repercussions. He liked it so much better when life followed the trajectory he'd graphed out in advance. With all the preparation and work he'd put into this deal, it didn't seem fair that unpredictable people were turning up to mess with his agenda.

Charlie got up and left his office. The library at the end of the hall was empty and he went in and closed the door. Thick, handwoven wool carpets cushioned his footsteps as he crossed to the bookcase next to the windows. He was tempted to pour himself some Scotch from the well-stocked bar hidden behind a walnut door set back in the shelves. He glanced at his watch. Nope. Still morning. No Scotch for him.

He pulled out his cell and called his brother.

"Hey," JT said.

"Hey."

The books on the shelf were out of alignment. What was the point of a library with leather-bound books if you weren't going to keep them straight? He pulled a few books forward and then ran his hand along the shelf, lining the rest of the spines up in perfect precision. He moved on to the next row.

"Charlie?"

"Yep."

"Was there a reason you called me?"

He stretched to reach the books on the shelf above his head.

"Do you remember that tournament Dad was in at the club when he was in the play-off against old Mr. Baxter?"

"Lauren's dad?"

"No. The grandfather."

"Oh, yeah. Dad broke his five iron when he missed the green on seventeen, didn't he? Smacked it off a tree and the damn thing snapped in half? Trip Dalton was working in the pro shop that summer, and he was taking bets on how many clubs Dad would break before the round ended."

"I was thinking about Baxter. There he was in the play-off and everyone was waiting for them to finish, Dad's throwing a fit, breaking clubs, and Baxter never changed. Kept his head up. Played his game. It was as if he wasn't even with Dad. Like he couldn't see him."

"That's right. The man was good. Never broke a sweat."

"That's why I want the partnership. You asked me why I'm working here. That's why."

Charlie had finished all the shelves on the left side of the window. He moved across to the other side of the room, but those books were in good shape. He slumped into one of the leather club chairs pulled up in front of the fireplace.

"Because Baxter was good at golf?"

"He didn't even need to be good at golf. He didn't need anything. Because he was part of this firm, he didn't need to be anything else. He was Old Man Baxter and that was all anyone needed to know. All hell could break loose around him and it wouldn't have mattered."

"Okay," JT said, but he sounded unsure.

"I don't like Lauren and Erik, but I'm not getting a partnership in them. It's this firm, this place."

JT sighed. "I get it, Charlie. But…" He hesitated. "What if you're too late? I mean, Baxter Smiley *is* Lauren and Erik now, right? Her granddad died."

"I have a lot invested here. Time. Work. Everything. Why should I start over just because Erik and Lauren are idiots?"

"You know what you're doing, Charlie. You always have."

JT hung up then and Charlie let his head fall back against the chair. If he knew what he was doing, why did he have these doubts? He looked around the quiet room.

He wanted this. So fine. He would do what he had to do to get it.

When he opened his office door, the phone was ringing. He lunged and grabbed it.

"Henry Ryan on line four for you," Madison said.

He wished he'd let it go to voice mail.

"Thanks." He switched to line four. "Charlie McNulty."

"Charlie, it's Henry."

"Good to hear from you," he said, managing to sound sincere if a little too hearty.

"Charlie, I'm calling you because I've always liked you," Henry said. If there was ever a sentence crying out for a "but," that was one. A pit opened in Charlie's stomach. "But I have to tell you, I've developed some reservations about Baxter Smiley in the past few weeks."

No. No, no, no, no. This call was not happening. Charlie paced to the far wall, feeling cramped inside his office.

"If you want me to come out and go over the plans I drew up for your portfolio, we can discuss any adjustments you're interested in, sir."

He'd reacted instinctively, trying to deflect Ryan when he should have let the man talk. The silence told him that he'd made a mistake. He held the phone tighter and pounded his fist on his thigh. He knew better than this. He *was* better than this.

"Charlie," Henry said, "I wasn't talking about the portfolio. Other guys can put the numbers together. You're supposed to be able to bring more than that."

Charlie nodded. Of course. When he'd approached Ryan, the pitch had been Baxter Smiley's reputation for discretion and loyalty. If people wanted to make buckets of money there were other places to go. Not that Charlie wouldn't do his best to make the Ryan family richer— he was good at making people richer. But the exclusive reputation of Baxter Smiley was what made this firm Ryan's top choice. What made it Charlie's top choice.

"My wife, Carol, she's been gone since the boys

were young. The school is her memory. Her monument. It's my tribute to her. Family matters."

"Yes, sir."

"Judging by recent events, I'm not sure Erik Finley understands this the way you do. Or I do."

Charlie swallowed. "He understands. I can assure you, sir, that what happened at the school was an aberration."

"I don't like to gossip, but I've heard disturbing rumors. Henry Junior was telling me last night about some incident with Erik's ex-wife?"

How did Henry Junior hear about that? Was he in the freaking ladies' room yesterday, too?

"Again, Henry, that was an unfortunate situation and one that will not happen again." At least not until Erik screwed around on Lauren.

"I see." But the tone of Ryan's voice implied that he didn't see at all.

That tone bothered Charlie. Ryan didn't know Sarah. It was easy to judge. Heck, Charlie had been judging right along with everybody else. But then, when he heard it from someone like Ryan or Kimberly, it made him mad.

"Henry, this has been a bad episode, but that's all it was. Baxter Smiley has a solid history. You and I are very close to finding terms that suit both of us, and that will further your long-term goals for your family. I'd hate to see any of this unfortunate, but thankfully isolated, incident affect those goals."

"I've said it before, Charlie. I like you. I'll be in touch."

"Yes, sir."

Henry Ryan hung up. Charlie cocked his arm as if

to throw the phone. But he drew a deep breath in and then released it. He made a quick circuit of his office and then another. Finally, he put the phone carefully back in the base.

He did not throw things. Erik and Lauren's soap opera might be messing up his biggest deal, his career-making deal. But they weren't going to make Charlie throw things.

THE KIDS WERE IN LINE for the kiddie train ride at Dorney Park. Sarah had one eye on them, but she was standing far enough away that they couldn't overhear her.

"I'm not talking to you until you take me off speaker and she gets out of the room," Sarah said. Erik had finally called her back. She hated speakerphones, you never knew who was eavesdropping, giggling with her hand over her mouth, making kissy faces at your ex-husband. Come to think of it, knowing exactly who was listening was even worse than not knowing.

"Have you lost your mind?" Erik snapped. "You pulled a knife on an elementary school principal and vandalized my place of business. Are you that jealous?"

As if.

"Take me off speaker, Erik." A pair of moms shepherding four toddlers had blocked her view of Lily and Simon so she moved to the left where she could see them again.

"Lauren has every right to hear this conversation," Erik said.

"Why, because she owns the boat?"

"No." Erik's voice was smug. "Because she's my wife. We got married last night."

Lauren giggled. She didn't even have her hand over her mouth. Sarah held the phone to her forehead and bit her lip. She'd suspected they were going to get married, but the very day the divorce was final?

"You got married on our anniversary?"

"I know, weird, right?" Erik said.

"We got married on your anniversary?" Lauren didn't sound as if she appreciated the irony. "You didn't think to mention that?"

"Honey, I was so excited about us, I didn't even remember until after we got the license."

Sarah said, "Get used to it, Second Mrs. Finley. He's not going to remember that it's your anniversary, either."

She heard a door slam in the background, and then Erik said, "That wasn't nice."

She was gratified he'd noticed. Simon and Lily climbed onto the train. Her daughter muscled a child out of the way to boost Simon into the seats directly behind the driver. *Go, Lily.*

"Marrying your new wife on my wedding anniversary wasn't nice, either, so I guess we're even."

"We're divorced," Erik said. "You don't have an anniversary anymore."

"Thank you for that information. Now I know why my roses never showed up."

"I don't appreciate this new tone, Sarah. Watch yourself at the hearing. Don't give the school any more reason to look sideways at our family."

The train pulled out of the fake train station and Sarah waved to the kids. Simon waved back. Lily was facing straight ahead, scoping out the track.

"The parts of our family that are actually showing up for the meeting are perfectly fine."

"Poor Madison at the front desk at Baxter Smiley would beg to differ on that point."

"Leave me out of it. We're talking about the kids. Neither of them assaulted anyone. There's absolutely no reason they shouldn't be welcomed back to school."

"Make sure you're on time. The kids need to dress up. Don't antagonize anyone."

He was wrapping things up. Probably had morning-after-the-wedding things to do. *Ew.*

She hated that she needed him, but she did. Or the kids did. She reached inside for the social voice she'd perfected over years of volunteering and committee work. "Erik, wait. Are you sure you can't make it back in time?"

"Positive. I'll be home next Sunday. We're taking an extra week for the honeymoon."

"The kids miss you. The only reason they brought the knife to school was that they thought you'd show up if they were in trouble."

"I can't be there, Sarah. Stop asking."

"What am I supposed to tell them?"

"Tell them I'll see them Sunday. And that I said to behave."

"Do you want to call them to tell them about the wedding?"

"I…" Eric cleared his throat. "I hadn't planned how to tell them. It came up suddenly."

The last little bit of compassion she had for him surfaced unexpectedly. He wasn't a strong man, so easily impressed by people with money or power, he was also easily led. From what she'd seen of Lauren over the years, the woman was a force of nature. He didn't stand a chance with her.

"Well, think about it before you get back. They need you," she said. "Did you know you missed Lily's baseball tryouts?"

"I called and pulled some strings," he said defensively. "She's on a good team."

As if Lily cared about some behind-the-scenes deal he'd made for her. She'd wanted him to be there, to show up and watch. Actually, she'd probably wanted both, and the opportunity to scheme with Erik about exactly which behind-the-scenes deal would most benefit her season.

"When you get back you have to take on the regular schedule like we planned. No more canceling."

"Why? Don't tell me you're dating someone?"

Oh, how she wanted to casually mention Charlie.

"They miss you, Erik. Maybe you could make some extra time to do something special, just with Simon."

"Like what?"

The way he asked, part skeptical, part taken aback, unnerved her.

"Figure it out. Just because we're divorced doesn't mean you can skip spending time with them."

"They have to start getting used to depending on you more," Erik said. "That's what being divorced is. I'm around, but not as much. I've still got work, and now Lauren—she wants to travel. My life is different now."

She didn't have any idea how to respond to what he'd just said. His selfishness and lack of compassion were astonishing. How long had he been disengaging from their family to have reached this level? He really expected her to say okay, that a less-than-part-time dad was perfect.

She was about to try to get him to see the kids' side of it, when he said, "I spoke to Charlie McNulty. He's on the board at the school and is close to Ryan. If he gets in touch and gives you any advice, make sure you listen."

"You what?"

"He's going to help smooth things over."

"Why would—" She stopped. "Forget it. See you when I see you."

Sarah closed the phone and turned it off as she walked over to the low wrought-iron fence, waiting for the train to chug back into view.

She felt sick to her stomach. Erik and Charlie had talked about her family behind her back? When? Had Charlie run home from Wilton's and called Erik? Maybe it had been earlier—that afternoon after he'd dropped her off but before they went out. She wondered if the dance had been part of the strategy. *God.* Would the new Mrs. Lauren Finley have been involved in the conversation? She could imagine it—the three of them on the phone, figuring out how to mitigate the fallout from the Unfortunate Incident with the Ex so their precious Baxter Smiley wouldn't be affected.

She made a fist and only then did she realize how angry she was. She would have expected to feel embarrassed or sorry for causing so much trouble. Instead she felt as if it would be a pretty good idea to wreck the office again. When she got home she just might download that

Carrie Underwood song about the chick with the Louis-ville Slugger beating up the cheater's car—would Erik have left his car at the airport? Would she be identifiable on the security camera if she wore a wig?

Luckily the train appeared at the far end of the track just then and she started waving and she didn't stop until the kids were out and back at her side.

"Who's up for Thunder Creek Mountain?" she asked. They had tickets to ride all day, and she intended to make the most of it.

There was plenty of time to plan for the school meeting, to figure out how to get the kids settled back into school. To decide what to do about her anger and how she was going to get Erik to be the dad her kids needed. But for today, if Erik or Charlie or Henry Ryan himself called, she was officially out of touch.

CHAPTER FIVE

ON MONDAY, SARAH TOOK the kids with her to Hailey's for the afternoon. Hailey had just started her leave from her physical therapy practice, and she was finalizing her preparations for the baby. The farmhouse she and JT had bought was the perfect place to forget her troubles. Lily had set herself up with her schoolbooks in Olivia's bedroom. Despite thinking Olivia needed a complete wardrobe and hair makeover focused primarily on adding what Lily called "fancy things," she had a serious case of hero worship for the older girl. Providing the opportunity to work at Olivia's desk was Sarah's way of soothing Lily's upset over being suspended.

The fourth-grade teacher, Mrs. Camp, had not made any promises on the zero front when Sarah called her, but neither had she denied the possibility of credit. Lily had decided to do her extra-best work to prove she was worthy.

Simon, who was delighted to be out of school and had shown no interest in keeping up with his work, was in the backyard playing catch by himself with one of JT's Frisbees. Hailey watched him through the kitchen window. He'd toss the Frisbee and then run as hard as he could, trying to get under it. She was surprised by how close he came a few times, but that was because his throws were generally short rather than because he was especially fast. Or good at catching.

"Is there something wrong with Simon?" Sarah asked.

Hailey leaned over the white enamel farmhouse sink to look out the window. "Why? Did he fall?"

"No. I mean, in general."

Hailey pushed the cotton curtains open all the way so they could watch him and then plunged her hands back into the warm water in the sink. She was washing a stack of tiny cotton T-shirts and sleep sacks. Sarah's job was to wring the garments out and lay them flat in the basket. Hailey wanted to hang them on the line to dry because, she'd told Sarah, she was looking forward to sniffing the baby.

Sarah had always enjoyed sniffing her own kids as newborns, so she was more than happy to help with the project. The warm, cozy, alive scent of their tiny bodies was one of the many things she'd liked about that age. The way they gripped her finger and held on tight. Their large heads that needed her hand to cover the soft spot and keep them safe. Being able to fix their troubles with a little rocking and a good nursing session. Lily and Simon had both been so needy but uncomplicated. Kissing their boo-boos really did make it all better. She missed babies.

"Simon is unique," Hailey said carefully.

"That's what I was afraid of."

She watched as he cocked the arm holding the Frisbee

so far behind his head that he fell over. He flipped on his stomach to examine something in the grass.

"Why are you thinking about him?" Hailey asked.

"I'm afraid the powers-that-be at the school want to cut him out of the herd."

Hailey raised a yellow striped T-shirt and rinsed it under the faucet. Sarah rolled the towel tightly around the T-shirt she was wringing. "Like a sick gazelle?"

"Like a kid who doesn't fit in."

"Sarah, he took a knife to school and the policy said they had to suspend him. Isn't that what the principal said?" Hailey handed her the next shirt.

Simon took off his left sneaker and brought it down quickly on a patch of grass in front of him. He lifted the heel slightly and peered under. Was he trying to catch something in his shoe? She hoped it was something nonpoisonous.

"Well, yeah, but I have a bad feeling."

"The disciplinary hearing is just a formality, I'm sure."

"But it's a private school. They make their own rules. They can do anything they want."

"If you want to find out what to expect, you could call Charlie. Or I can get JT to do it."

"Do not call Charlie," Sarah said. "Erik already dragged him into this."

"Why?"

"He says he has influence with Henry Ryan or something. If he calls me before the hearing I'm supposed to do what he tells me."

"And this bothers you," Hailey said, handing her the yellow shirt.

"Yes, it bothers me. Charlie is a grown man and I'm a grown woman. Neither of us is related to the other and he shouldn't be calling me to tell me what to do."

"But he hasn't called you, has he?"

"No," Sarah said. He hadn't called about that, which was a very good thing, and if it had been by choice, well, she approved. On the other hand, he hadn't called about…anything else. Like that kiss. She rolled the shirt up in the towel, squeezing tight so her hands would be occupied and she wouldn't touch her cheek where he'd kissed her. It had been an innocent peck, nothing more. That she was still dwelling on it meant more about her recent lack of male attention than it did about anything between her and Charlie. Because there wasn't anything between her and Charlie except an enormous mess.

"So that probably means everything is fine."

"Or maybe it means he doesn't want to tell me that he found out they're expelling the kids."

"If he thought expulsion was a possibility he'd call. That deal matters to him. JT says he believes if he makes partner at Baxter Smiley his life will be perfect forever."

Sarah squeezed the towel hard, giving it a vicious twist. "Because being part of Lauren's team is everyone's life goal."

Hailey gave her a sympathetic look. She'd been appropriately outraged by the wedding when she'd heard.

"It's just Charlie. You know their childhood was so nuts, Sarah. He's warped about stability," she said as she glanced out the window. "There's nothing to worry about. Simon's fine. He's not getting expelled from first grade. It's an elementary school, not a pack of cheetahs. I'm sure his place in the herd is secure."

CHARLIE DIDN'T CALL. Sarah decided that was all right with her. If she had heard from him, she'd have been looking for ulterior motives or coded messages sent from Lauren and Erik's love nest. Much better to make a clean break. Not that there'd been anything going on to make a break from. But…still.

On the morning of the school meeting, she was up early and had her breakfast on the patio, purposely trying to find her old comfort in her old routines. She'd gone over and around on every angle she could think of and she'd decided the best thing was for the kids to go back to their school. There were other schools they could go to, but she didn't want them to experience the failure of being expelled. If everything could just go back the way it had been that would be the best outcome.

For this meeting she'd pulled out all the stops, and not because Erik told her to. She knew as well as he did what was required to fit in with the fine families at Carol Ryan Memorial. She wasn't just wearing a scarf, she'd dug out a pair of panty hose and a slip. Her brown skirt was serious, her red jacket was confident, and the white silk shirt said that although she was taking the hearing to heart at the end of the day, she had no concerns about the outcome. At least she hoped that was what it said. She put her diamond studs in, just in case.

Lily had chosen the sweet high-waisted yellow dress

she'd worn at Easter. Her blond hair was pulled back in a neat ponytail. The yellow-and-white-checked ribbon bow might have been too much on some other accused terrorist, but Lily had so many years of experience at being loved and successful, it worked perfectly for her. Respectability oozed out of her pores.

She kissed her daughter and sent her downstairs to wait. She didn't even have to say "Don't get dirty." Dirt wouldn't dare approach Lily Finley today.

Sarah stuck her head in Simon's room and, when she saw what he was wearing, had to duck back out again while she struggled to get her laughter under control. She was so on edge there was every chance the inappropriate laugh would show up and she couldn't afford that today.

Once she was composed, she went into his room, picking her way carefully around the Lego moon-landing scene laid out near the door. Simon was a collector, which meant the flat surfaces in his room, bookcase, windowsill—even the floor in front of the dresser—displayed objects he'd made or found.

His interests morphed periodically, but he was never able to let go of the last collection, so it was possible to track his developing mind from rain forest animals, through giants, and on to gears, pulleys and the solar system. JT's robotics company was involved in a project with NASA and he'd given Simon two detailed modeling kits. A miniature—but to scale—model of the planets hung in front of each window. She felt a pang when she realized it had been JT, not Erik, who'd helped put the models together.

Her son was sitting on the edge of his top bunk, his feet dangling. He'd put on the khaki pants, blue pin-stripe oxford and penny loafers she'd set out for him, but he'd added one of Erik's old ties. It must have come from the dress-up basket or possibly the Goodwill bag because it was a holiday-theme tie patterned with large cartoon reindeer that Erik wouldn't have worn on a bet.

If you pressed the right spot at the bottom, the tie played a tinny version of "Up on the Housetop." She'd bought it for him when Lily was little, thinking he might get a kick out of sharing it with their daughter. As far as she knew, he'd never put it on, not even in the house. Lily had carried it around that Christmas season, playing the song for anyone she could trap into listening. Sarah hadn't seen it since.

The tie was too long, and while Simon had given a Windsor knot his best shot, the resulting wad of fabric at his neck made him look like he had a green-and-red goiter.

His face was freshly washed, but glum.

"What's going on, buddy? Are you nervous?"

"No."

She came all the way into the room and touched his left foot. "You don't look happy."

"I'm not."

"Want to talk about it?"

"No," Simon said.

"Oh." Sarah was trying to figure out how to get him to open up when he elaborated.

"I mean, no I don't want to talk about it and that's the problem," Simon said. "When you go to see the principal they ask you why you did stuff and what you were thinking and sometimes I don't *know* what I was thinking but this time I do know. I know exactly. Except I don't want to talk about it. Because it's Dad."

Sarah reached for him. He was six, getting too big for her to pick him up, but he slid off the bunk bed and into her arms. He put his face down into her neck and she sniffed his soft hair, the combination of apple-scented shampoo and boy that was so utterly him. *Simon*. Her baby. So sweet. So smart. He deserved better from the grown-ups around him.

"You don't have to talk about Dad if it makes you sad. I'll be right there."

He lifted his head, affronted. "I'm not sad about Dad. I'm mad at him. Me and Lily came up with a plan to make him come home. We did the whole plan and Lily even got suspended, which she hates, and she's not getting perfect attendance and might even have a *zero*. And he still didn't come."

"Okay," Sarah said. "I can see how you'd be mad about those things."

"So if they ask me why I took a knife to school I'm not going to say why," Simon said. He pushed her away. "They already call me freak, anyway. I can say I brought it because I'm a freak."

He was heading for the door, but she stopped him. "Simon?"

He turned to her. She wanted to pick him up again. To tell him he didn't have to go to the hearing. To tell him to point out who'd called him a freak so she could kill them. But none of that would help him right now.

She did know these people, what they wanted and

how they judged. She could at least help him look like what they expected for the hearing. So they wouldn't be able to call him a freak today. He'd be taken back along with Lily and they could all go on with their lives as if this had never happened.

There wasn't a lot on the list of things Sarah was good at, but fitting in and making people like her were close to the top. She could show Simon how to do it. Survival skills for the second-best.

"The tie was a good idea," she said, careful not to hurt his feelings. "Makes you look responsible. But that particular tie, because it's Dad's, well, it's too long for you. I think for this meeting we should skip it." Sarah loosened the knot and helped him pull it over his head. She looped it over his doorknob in case he wanted to put it back on later. "Maybe next time we'll get a tie that's your size."

"No next time, Mom. I'm not doing this again."

She took his hand and led him out of the room, turning the lights off as they went. This might be the last time Simon would be explaining a weapon in school, but she had a horrible feeling it was far from the last time he'd be asked to explain himself.

WHEN THEY GOT TO THE SCHOOL, Sarah parked in a visitor space and they went inside. It was just before the second lunch period and the hallway was packed with fourth- and fifth-graders lining up for the cafeteria. A sudden quiet fell over the crowd, broken by a giggle and someone's whispered "It's the Finleys."

Simon scowled but pressed closer to her. Lily's back stayed straight and her smile didn't waver, but somehow, her bright, impermeable aura of success seemed punctured. Dimmed. Sarah could have kicked herself. Why was this appointment during school hours? She was so far out of her depth here, it hadn't occurred to her that they'd have to walk this gauntlet of children.

She spotted Cindi, a girl who played pitcher on Lily's baseball team and who'd been to their house countless times. She waved to her and said, "Hi, Cindi." Cindi didn't respond but moved out of sight behind a tall boy.

Sarah was never so happy to see the principal's office. The door to the outer office swished shut behind them and she heard Lily's quick exhalation, the kind of breath a person might let out after finishing a set of lifts at the gym.

Ted's door was closed. Jessica looked up from the computer. "He's in a meeting." She gestured to the row of chairs near the wall. "You can sit there while you wait."

Sarah sat with the children on either side of her. Ordinarily she'd have chatted with Jessica, but she was getting a definite do-not-approach vibe from the other woman. The rumble of male voices coming from Ted's office grew louder as she heard the distinct sound of a chair being pushed back.

When the inner door opened, she blushed to see Henry Ryan emerge, followed by Charlie, who was facing away from her, holding his hand out to Ted.

As she watched, Ted grasped Charlie's right hand in both of his. He pumped up and down with his usual friendly vigor. "This was great, fellas. Until the board meeting next week."

Then he saw her and the kids sitting on the bench, and Ted's beaming smile faltered.

Why hadn't they scheduled this appointment for later in the day? After hours? Off-site, even? She hunched back into her seat, hoping Henry and Charlie would walk right on by without seeing her.

Simon said in a stage whisper to Lily, "That's Mr. Henry Ryan. He's the husband of Mrs. Carol Ryan Memorial."

"That's not her name," Lily whispered back.

"Yes, it is, too. Her picture is on the front of the school."

Lily put her hand over his mouth. "Shut. Up."

Too late. All three men turned toward them. Henry Ryan was a tall man, even taller than Charlie. He was thin—skinny, really—with a long face and a full head of iron-gray hair he wore in an unflattering squared-off style she would have been willing to bet he trimmed at home with kitchen shears. If he'd claimed Abraham Lincoln as an ancestor, it would have been wholly believable.

He crossed the office toward them. "Sarah Finley?"

She stood up. Charlie was dressed in his full banker's rig today—a sharp navy suit with a faint gray stripe. Yet he seemed uncomfortable.

"Sarah," Ryan said. "I think we may have met before. As the young man mentioned, I'm Henry Ryan."

She took his hand, his long, thin fingers wrapping around hers with disconcerting strength. "It's a pleasure to see you again," she said, even as she wished he would head right on out of the office.

Unfortunately, he didn't move along.

"You're feeling better today?"

She wasn't sure what he meant.

"I heard about your…incident at the office."

"Oh." How mortifying. She did not, would not look at Charlie. "Yes. Feeling fine now."

"Good."

She was hyperaware of her children sitting behind her. If she were a mother killdeer, she'd be faking a broken wing right about now, convincing this man to move away from her babies. Instead, he gave each child a measured look, making it seem he was sizing them up for uniforms. Maybe straitjackets. "These are your children?" he asked.

Sarah nodded and then nudged them to their feet. She didn't like that he was judging the children. They didn't have anything to hide from Henry Ryan or anyone else. "Lily, Simon, say hello to Mr. Ryan."

The children greeted him politely.

"Do you like going to this school?" he asked.

Lily nodded vigorously. Simon shrugged and Sarah's heart beat faster. She knew Ryan noticed his lack of commitment.

"Simon, you didn't answer the question," he said.

"I like the library. And art. But I really don't like gym and the cafeteria smells funny. The picture of Mrs. Carol Ryan Memorial is pretty." He shot a superior look at his sister, pleased that he'd managed to fit in that piece of information.

Ryan's thin lips compressed. Sarah couldn't interpret what he was thinking as he studied Simon for a few long seconds. Finally he said, "My wife liked children. Most of all she liked little boys. She would be happy to hear you like your art class."

Simon didn't answer him. Charlie stepped forward

and put a hand on Ryan's arm. "I'm heading back to the office. Thanks for the meeting."

"Hi, Mr. McNulty," Simon said. "Did you have to talk to the principal about going in the girls' room?"

Charlie looked startled, but then he recovered. "It was something different."

Ryan said to the kids, "Have a good chat with the principal, then, and do what he tells you so you can keep coming here, right?"

Lily nodded again. Charlie smiled, but Sarah couldn't tell what he meant by it. How many times was he going to be a witness to her worst moments?

When the two men had left, Ted motioned her in. As she walked across the office, she noticed Jessica's hand on her phone. Sarah let the children precede her into the office and then took a step inside herself. She waited half a second, then turned back and made eye contact with Jessica. She gave her the don't-you-dare look she usually reserved for Simon and Lily when they were about to cross a line. Jessica dropped her hand away from the phone.

Sarah closed the door behind her and sat between her children.

"Before I tell you what we've discussed, I'd like to hear from the children," Ted said. "Simon, can you tell us why you brought the knife to school?"

Simon gave his mother a quick look and then he shook his head. "No, thank you."

Ted leaned closer to him. "We'd like to understand why you did this, Simon, so we can decide how to help you and your sister."

"Oh. To help us." Simon folded his hands on his lap. "Well, Lily wants her zeros erased, and if she could get perfect attendance back that would be nice, too. I don't need anything."

Sarah bit the inside of her cheek so she wouldn't laugh.

"That wasn't the kind of helping I meant." Ted cleared his throat. "Lily? Can you tell us why Simon had the knife at school?"

"My brother and I are very sorry that he brought a knife to school. We know it was wrong and we promise never to do anything like that again. We didn't mean to hurt anybody and we are glad that didn't happen, not even accidentally." She sucked in a breath and continued with her clearly rehearsed speech. "We've used our suspension time to think about our actions, and we promise that if you'll allow us to rejoin the school community we are ready to be exceptional Carol Ryan Memorial students."

Sarah stared at her daughter. She could give lessons to *politicians*. She hadn't answered Ted's question, had thrown all the blame on Simon and then had voiced a completely cloying apology without a hint that she meant it in any but the most sincere way. Ted took his pen out and made notes in one of the files on his desk.

"Mrs. Finley, maybe you'd like to tell us what you think?" he said.

What she thought was Lily was going to be fine even if she had to go to school in a piranha tank.

"Is there any way you could call me Sarah?" she asked.

Ted nodded uncertainly.

She almost crossed her legs but remembered that

could be seen as a defensive posture. "My children made a mistake, but it had very little to do with the knife and absolutely nothing to do with hurting anyone. If this hearing is to determine if they're likely to cause violence at the school, I'm quite positive that neither of them are dangerous and would never dream of hurting a classmate."

"I'm not sure how you can say bringing a knife to school isn't about violence."

"He only took it out of his backpack so the teacher would see it and send him to the office. Showing it off was part of their plan."

"Okay," Ted said, making another note. Maybe she shouldn't have said that.

"Let me tell you what we've decided," he said. "I spoke with some of the other faculty and I've received some input from the board." He gestured toward the door and she felt her hands curl into fists. Charlie and Henry Ryan. "We've decided to extend the suspension for a month. At the end of the suspension, the children will be allowed to return to school on probation. They'll sign a behavior modification pledge, basically requiring them to agree to abide by the standards already established for students at the school. If they live up to those standards for the following year, the probation will be lifted."

"I'm sorry," Sarah said. "That's a lot to take in."

Part of her was relieved. If the kids could come back, wasn't that what she wanted? But then some of Ted's words were circling in her mind: *probation, behavior pledge, standards.*

Ted cleared his throat. "Mrs. Finley, we understand that your family may be in some difficult circumstances just now. You might want to look into counseling while you and your husband work out your issues."

"Ex," Sarah said.

"Pardon me?"

"Erik is my ex-husband." She stood up. She should thank the principal, have the children thank him, but she wasn't ready for that. She needed time.

"We'll send you the official discipline plan in the next three days. You and your…Mr. Finley have to sign it and send it back."

Lily looked as if she wanted to say something, but Sarah opened the door and she and Simon followed her out, past Jessica and through the glass doors into the lobby. She realized her hands were shaking and her skin felt clammy. She wasn't angry… Was it shock? She didn't know what she was feeling.

Luckily her car was right there and they could climb in and go home, far from the Carol Ryan Memorial school and everyone involved with it, until she figured out what was going on.

Except Charlie was there. His Mercedes was in the spot next to hers and he was leaning on the passenger-side door, staring at his BlackBerry. When he saw them, he slid it into his pocket and straightened.

"Everything okay?" he asked with a confident smile.

"No," she said, her voice uneven.

Charlie's forehead wrinkled. "What do you mean?"

She unlocked the car. "Get in," she said to the kids. She waited until they'd climbed in and then closed the door after them. Then she walked away, down the row of visitor spaces. Charlie followed her.

"I thought everything was taken care of," he said. "What happened?"

"What happened?" Sarah repeated. "Ted suspended them for a month, at which point he will graciously allow them to come back to school if they sign a behavior pledge and agree to toe the line for an entire year. Basically, they have to agree to be scrutinized for any signs of abnormality for the next twelve months."

Charlie nodded, as if he were ticking off the points as she said them. "Right," he said when she'd finished.

"Of course, this isn't news to you because apparently you've been providing *input*."

"Erik asked me to—"

"Don't," she said. "You had no right."

"But, Sarah, they can come back to school. What's the problem?"

She raised her hands in front of her as if to stop his words from coming through. "I don't know what the problem is, exactly. I just know that this is my family and you and Erik and Henry Ryan have your business mixed up in it somehow and that's not okay with me."

He stiffened. "Erik told me to get involved."

"I heard," Sarah said, the words coming out with more force than she expected. "I'm sorry you're in the middle of this, but you shouldn't have done that. He shouldn't have asked you to, but you should have told him no."

"I'm on the board."

"There are other board members."

"It's not like I had a lot of choices," he said. "Someone needed to get this thing under control."

"You have to be joking. I had it under control. I'm their mother."

"You? You had it under control when you let Simon bring a knife to school or when you had a public fit that Ryan heard about?"

She was so stung she felt as if he'd slapped her.

"That was a very bad day for us, Charlie. I don't understand how that one day—one, out of all the other days I've been an exemplary member of this school community—trumps everything else. It's not as if I'm planning to make a career out of smashing dishes."

"Well, since you brought careers into this, maybe you can see my position." His voice was softer, laced with what she thought was a plea. "I'm up for a partnership vote this spring, and if Erik or Lauren tells me a particular client is important, I've got to take care of that."

"Even if it means butting into my life where you don't belong?"

"I thought I was helping," he said, his jaw clenched. "I meant to be helpful."

"I don't need help. I'm fine."

CHAPTER SIX

HE'D BEEN SO CAUGHT UP in trying to make Sarah understand, Charlie hadn't noticed a car parking a few spaces down. He heard a door slam but didn't look up until a voice called over his shoulder, "Sarah! Just the person I needed to see."

They both jerked around. Danielle Simmons was behind them, her hot-pink Crocs having made no sound on the pavement as she approached.

Danielle was the PTA president, and from what Charlie had gleaned at the board meetings she attended, she took her duties as an all-around expert mother/volunteer/fundraiser seriously.

"Hi, Danielle," Sarah said. He had to give her credit for a quick recovery.

"The teacher appreciation luncheon is tomorrow, as you know."

Sarah nodded.

"And we've been planning on your fantastic strawberry shortcakes as usual." She included Charlie in her smile. "They're delightful! Individual servings with fresh whipped cream, each one garnished with a twist of mint. The staff love them. She makes them every year."

"I…I'm not sure…"

"Obviously." Danielle's gaze slid to Charlie and then back to Sarah. "You can't be expected to serve at the luncheon this year. Not with everything that's happened." She shrugged and said in a singsong voice, "Awkward."

"O-kay," Sarah said.

"So I can pick everything up the morning of. Plan for one hundred and ten because people will want seconds. Does that work?"

Sarah blinked. "Does what work?"

"That you'll make the strawberry shortcakes and I'll pick them up. You could deliver them, I guess, but I wouldn't want to make the teachers…uncomfortable." Danielle patted Sarah's arm. "Will the mint wilt if you assemble them at home?"

Sarah didn't look like she was swallowing this plan very well. Charlie didn't blame her, but he watched her face, waiting for the attack he knew was on its way.

"I don't think I'll be able to make the strawberry shortcakes this year," Sarah said. She didn't sound nuts. Not yet, anyway.

"You signed up," Danielle protested.

"I'm—" She paused and Charlie braced himself for an outburst. "Busy," she finished.

The other woman's perfectly plucked brows drew down. "We don't have time to recruit someone else, Sarah. You have to do it."

"No," she said. "I don't."

She patted her purse. He remembered she'd done the same thing that day in the office when she was pulling herself together.

"You can make your own damn strawberry short-cakes. Or how about the teachers skip dessert? Improve their moral fiber?" Sarah said. "Or better yet, maybe Charlie will help you. He's very interested in the school these days." She turned on her heel and walked back to her car. Danielle scowled after Sarah.

"You signed up!" she yelled.

"Psyche!" Sarah yelled back.

Danielle stamped a pink Croc and growled. Then she looked at him, considering, finger poised over the screen of her iPhone. She couldn't possibly—

"Do you cook, Charlie?"

He sighed and reached into his pocket for his check-book. "No. But I order out."

CHARLIE HATED GROCERY shopping. He hated the carts with their rattling wheels and the way everyone could see what you were buying.

It wasn't that he didn't like to eat. He loved to eat. But he didn't like to cook. So to avoid having to stock his own kitchen, he ate takeout, mooched meals at JT and Hailey's and even suffered through the occasional dinner with his dad, who had mellowed after JT's marriage, but was still contrary and annoying when he wanted. It seemed like a huge waste of time to bother cooking for one person. But once every two months or so he was forced to grocery shop for more than what he could pick up at the 7-Eleven on the corner. Today had been that day. He was thankful it was over, but still hadn't quite shed the bad mood shopping always gave him.

He was driving past Sarah's house with the backseat of his car full of bags of toilet paper, coffee beans, beer and lightbulbs. Her house wasn't technically on his way home, but he told himself he was avoiding traffic, another Saturday-morning annoyance, with this detour.

The first water balloon hit his windshield with such a tremendous noise he thought his tire had blown. He jerked the wheel, waiting for the drag from the skid, but then the water dripping down from the top of the window and the fragments of colored latex registered. He pulled into the next parking spot on the street.

What the hell?

He got out and slammed the door, planning to read the riot act to whatever juvenile delinquent was stupid enough to be chucking missiles at cars.

He stared up and down the street, but he didn't see anyone. Of course, they were hiding. Well, he would just wait them out.

Splat.

Another balloon, pink, landed on the sidewalk at his feet, the cold water splashing his sneakers and the hem of his jeans.

Unfortunately for the delinquents, he'd seen where that one came from. The front porch of that big… He stopped. It was Sarah's house.

What the hell?

She stuck her head around one of the porch pillars and waved to him. "Did we get you?"

"Yes, yes, you did!" he hollered, bewildered. The last time he'd seen her she'd been pissed at him, pulling out of the school parking lot while he wrote a check to the

PTA for six-dozen pastries. Now she was throwing water balloons at him?

Sarah turned to someone behind her, and then he saw Simon lean out and wave to him, "Hi, Mr. McNulty!"

"Come say hi," Sarah called to Charlie. "Unless you're chicken."

He had no choice but to go up and talk to them. He kicked at the shredded balloon at his feet, but he was having trouble hanging on to his bad mood.

Sarah and Simon were laughing together. Each of them was wearing a bandanna and carrying more water balloons in each hand. He spotted a pack of balloons sticking out of the back pocket of Sarah's blue shorts. The curve of her ass and her slender, muscular legs distracted him from his anger even more. He managed to look away. For about three seconds.

"We totally got you," Simon said. "Mom did the throwing, but I got the timing!"

"You threw the balloon?" he asked. "What if it hadn't been me but some old lady and she had a heart attack?"

Sarah made a face. "We knew it was you," she said. "You don't seriously think we'd toss a water balloon at just anybody, do you?"

"You…you targeted me?" He couldn't believe that she thought that made it better. What kind of irresponsible person encouraged her son to toss water balloons at—

"Yep, we aimed right for you," Simon said. "We like you."

"You…" His protest evaporated in the face of Simon's smile. "That's how you show people you like them?"

Simon nodded. "It's one way," he said slowly, as if

he were working through the implications as he spoke. "But it wouldn't be a good way for some people." Then he brightened. "Good thing it was a good way for you."

Sarah didn't look nearly as confident about that as her son. She put her arm around his neck in a protective gesture that made Charlie feel like a six-ton jerk. It was just a water balloon. Yeah, he'd never have encouraged the kid to throw it, but it was kind of funny. And no one had gotten hurt.

He looked back down at Simon. *They liked him?* He met Sarah's eyes. She was watching him, her jaw set.

"Simon likes you," she corrected. "The jury is still out with me."

"I said I was sorry for butting in."

"I don't actually think you did," she said. "I think you said I should be grateful that someone was taking control."

"Well, I am sorry. I shouldn't have said that. It's just…" Just that when Sarah was around he was never in control of himself the way he liked. He couldn't say that to her, though. "Just that I made a mistake."

She went still as she studied him. He squelched the impulse to squirm like a third-grader caught talking in the library. He was surprised how much it mattered that she wasn't mad at him anymore.

"Apology accepted," Sarah said.

"You want to throw water balloons?" Simon asked. "We're having a war."

He was trying to figure out what he should say next, how to get out of the situation without hurting Simon's feelings, when a piercing yell erupted from the bushes next to the porch and five or six water balloons exploded on the porch around them. One hit Charlie square in the back and he saw another explode on Sarah's hip.

"Who the hell was that?" he yelled.

"That was the war!" Simon said as he and his mom dove for the steps, tossing their balloons back into the bushes. A group of howling kids exploded out of them and took off around the other side of the house. Sarah looked back at him. "Sorry about making you stop. I thought it would be funny. I guess you're probably busy today."

Simon had disappeared around the corner, and Charlie heard more hysterical screaming coming from the back of the house. Sarah looked so alive to him, her strong legs poised to push off from the steps, blond curls gathered at the back of her head under the bandanna, her eyes lit up with fun. Was he actually turning into the old guy who hollered at kids for throwing water balloons? What was next? Handing out toothbrushes at Halloween?

He could remember the thrill of hide-and-seek when he was a kid and the many epic wars he and JT had waged with their water guns. He'd hardly had time for a game of horse the past two years, let alone a water balloon fight.

And he still had grocery-shopping mood to work through. Plus he was pretty sure it had been the kid in the green shirt who had nailed him. That child was in need of some lessons about respecting his elders.

"Where's the hose?" he asked.

She grinned at him. "Seriously? You were mad."

"I am mad. Your kid got me square. I have to avenge my honor." If avenging his honor came with the side benefit of an hour spent in her company, watching her smile, listening to her laugh, getting a better look at her very nice legs, well, a man had to do what a man had to do. This was war, after all.

"Hose is on the patio. There's also a garbage can of full balloons there and another one beside the carriage house. Pool area is off-limits. Try not to yell any more curse words—some of these kids are sensitive."

"Sorry about that."

"Clean slate," she said. "Let's both start over." Then she stuck her tongue out at him. "The water in those suckers is cold enough to make anyone let loose a little profanity."

He pushed the keys down in the pocket of his jeans and trotted down the porch steps. She was waiting for him at the corner of the house.

"Oh, and, Charlie?" She raised an eyebrow. "Anyone who tracks mud in the house isn't getting any ice cream."

Then she lifted her hand and he realized she was still holding a balloon. She looked from his face to his chest, her eyes dancing.

"You wouldn't dare," he said, hoping he was wrong.

"Oh, I would dare," she said, moving a step closer and reaching out to press the balloon against his shirt, testing the strength. It took everything he had not to put his arms around her. She was so alive, so full of the devil, he wanted to grab her and…

She stepped back. "I would dare," she said. Did she sound out of breath? "But you're unarmed. So I can't."

She didn't give him a chance to answer, just took off running around the house.

The fight ranged from the front yard to the back. Before too long, Charlie got a solid shot in on Simon, who shrieked and fell over. When he ran up to see if the boy was hurt, Simon pulled a squirt gun out of his pocket and got him in the face. Unfortunately for the boy, a childhood spent with JT had taught Charlie a thing or two about hand-to-hand combat, and with his three-to-one size advantage, he was soon in possession of the gun and the back of Simon's neck was dripping icy water down his shirt.

Charlie didn't feel guilty. Simon didn't look distressed.

Sarah couldn't believe Charlie had stayed. She wasn't even sure why she'd thrown the balloon at his car. Wanting to make Simon happy, sure. But if she were honest, she'd admit it had a lot more to do with wanting to see Charlie, to see if he'd stop, to see if he'd stay. She wasn't entirely sure she trusted him after the way he'd stuck his nose into their business, but his explanation about the partnership made sense.

She crouched down behind the chaise on the patio, trying to keep Lucas Patterson from plugging her with what he swore was the coldest balloon yet. She peered out from between two potted ferns, hoping Lucas would find another victim.

Charlie ran out from behind the carriage house, Simon in hot pursuit. Simon reared back and threw his balloon at Charlie, but it went zinging off sideways, nowhere close to the target. She'd seen that happen more often than not when Simon threw today. He hadn't gotten even a whisker of Lily's natural athletic talent. Charlie spun around and threw a balloon back at her son, but he missed, too. She suspected he'd made a bad throw on purpose. No ex–state champion quarterback could have missed at that range.

She was about to leave her hiding spot when she saw Charlie put his hands up in an "I surrender" gesture. He approached Simon and she could see them chatting. Charlie moved behind Simon and helped him square his shoulders and his hips, point his toe and cock his arm. Then Charlie walked him through stepping into the throw. Simon grabbed a new balloon just as Lucas ran past and, using his new form—or at least an approximation of his new form—got a direct hit on the other boy. Lucas immediately pelted Charlie and Simon, but they were too busy high-fiving each other to care.

She sank back on her heels, glad for the cover of the chair and the ferns. What she'd just seen was so sweet and so unexpected, and so exactly what Simon needed. Lauren better give him his partnership, she thought. She didn't deserve Charlie, but she better give it to him.

At one point he had a group of three kids, two girls and a boy, pinned down in the bushes near the patio. They were a little older than Simon and had put up a good fight, but they ran out of ammo. He was sitting in an Adirondack chair, a bucket of balloons at his side, amusing himself by pegging them anytime a body part appeared. The kids would screech and retreat to regroup. He was wondering how long it would take for them to figure out they'd be home free if they rushed him in a bunch when he heard a stealthy crunch of gravel behind him. He turned but Sarah and Simon were too close. And they had the hose.

The spray hit his face and he swallowed a mouthful of

cold, metallic hose water. The kids he'd had pinned sprinted out of the bushes, stealing balloons from his ammo bucket and pelting him from three sides. In less than ten seconds he was totally soaked and begging for mercy.

Sarah turned off the hose, and they were about to enter into a negotiated peace that would eventually have included that promised ice cream when a woman walked up the driveway, shouting, "Lucas Patterson! What are you doing?"

The boy who'd been pinned down in the bushes jumped and walked toward her. Another woman appeared behind the first one and a girl with a brown bob and a thoroughly muddy pair of shorts said, "Oh, no."

Sarah turned to greet the women, the hose in her hand dripping on the driveway. Charlie slicked his hands through his hair and water trailed down the underside of his arms and the back of his shirt. He tried to discreetly unstick the fabric from his chest, but the second woman saw him. He dropped his hand.

"What is going on here, Sarah?" the first woman demanded. She had short red hair and a pair of expensive-looking oversize sunglasses.

The kids moved into a tight group behind Charlie. He didn't see Simon.

"We're having a water balloon fight," Sarah said evenly. She shook her foot and water flew out of her sneaker, spattering the redhead's sandal.

"Roger was driving home and he said someone was throwing water balloons at cars."

"That was me. The kids were only throwing them at one another."

The second woman gasped as she grabbed for the muddy girl's hand. He finally placed her. Tina Roland—she lived around the corner with her husband, a heart surgeon.

"When you called to ask if Jen could come over," Tina said, "I am positive I said no. How do you explain her being here?"

"We don't allow weapons play, Lucas," the first woman said. "You know better."

Tina added, "You'd think Sarah would know better. Especially while the children are suspended. You don't care about the example you're setting?"

"They're not actually weapons," Sarah said. "It's more water play than weapons play."

This was going nowhere fast. Tina and Lucas's mom were obviously spoiling for a fight, and Sarah didn't seem inclined to back down or to apologize. Charlie was trying to figure out if there was something he could do or say to defuse the argument when a water balloon sailed over the wall of the patio and landed smack in between Tina and her friend. They jumped backward, furious.

"Well," Tina said.

"Exactly." Lucas's mom tugged his hand. "We're going home and Lucas is not to come back here." She paused, eyeing the group behind Charlie. "Patrick and Rachel, I'm sure your mother will want to know what you've been up to, as well."

As the moms went down the driveway, the remaining few kids melted away with muttered "Thanks, Mrs. Finley."

Sarah waited until they'd all gone and then called, "Simon, you can come out now."

He climbed over the wall from the patio and trudged toward them. Charlie should have headed out, let them have their privacy, but he didn't want to interrupt.

"That was rude, Simon," she said.

The boy ducked his head and said softly, "Sorry."

Neither of them said anything for a second. Charlie didn't know what he expected. Some kind of reprimand. Sarah had gotten pretty thoroughly chewed out. In Charlie's experience, that meant she'd probably pass the favor along to her kid.

"Good aim, though," she said.

Simon's head came up, his eyes lit with mischief. "They shouldn't have yelled at you."

Sarah ruffled his hair. "Some people don't understand fun." The boy grinned at her, and Charlie wondered what it felt like to have a kid trust you that completely. "Why don't you check around the yard for the water guns and we'll get things cleaned up a bit."

Simon nodded and took off.

Charlie said, "I better get home, too." Now that the adrenaline was draining away, he felt stiff. Embarrassed. He wasn't sure what had possessed him to get involved in the game in the first place.

"We're having pizza," Sarah said. "If you want to stay."

He couldn't. It wasn't only that Sarah and Simon and the confrontation with the mothers had reminded him uncomfortably of his own childhood, when his mother had broken just about every social convention and rule there was and he and JT had frequently been dragged into the mess with her. It was that he couldn't afford to get mixed up with Sarah. She and Erik and Lauren had created enough of a soap opera at the firm. He didn't need people like Tina seeing him here and reporting back to Erik or Lauren, or even Henry Ryan. He couldn't afford to get on anyone's bad side before the partnership negotiations were finished.

Getting involved with Sarah meant he might as well kiss his partnership goodbye. He had too much time and effort invested to risk it by eating pizza with Sarah and her son. No matter how good she looked with her clothes soaked to her skin and her hair curling from the water.

"I better go," he said again. But then he didn't go. He reached out with two fingers and wiped a spot of muddy water off her collarbone, just above the V-neck of her shirt. Her skin was warm and smooth, and it was all he could do not to keep moving his hand down, inside the neck of her shirt. She went still under his hand. Maybe…no. There was one right thing to do and that was to go. Now.

She shivered as he backed up. The hose in her hand was still dripping water; maybe she was simply cold. He started to walk away.

"Lily is gone to a birthday party." Her voice was soft, each word gentle, as if she were puzzling over the meaning. "Simon wasn't invited. Nobody said why, but he's always been invited to this child's party before and he knows it. He might have problems following the rules, but there is nothing wrong with his memory. I was just trying to cheer him up."

Charlie looked around the yard where the remains of

the water balloon fight were scattered. "He had a good time, Sarah."

"He did." She sounded more confident now. "When I talked to Tina about having her daughter come over, and by the way, Jen showed up on her own, I did not go around like some Pied Piper of weapons play and steal kids from their yards—she made me mad. Telling me what I should be doing to 'repair my reputation and that of the children.'"

Charlie nodded. He wasn't sure what to say.

"My kids made a mistake. And I lost my temper. Once. As a family, we had one bad day. And since then, Simon's getting cut out of the birthday lists, kids are getting banned from our yard. Danielle says I'll make the teachers uncomfortable if I serve them their precious dessert. I swear, Charlie, I'm tired of this. It's like if you don't fit into exactly the right hole, you're done. Makes me want to stop trying."

She had a point. But still. "People like to know what to expect."

"Did you ever throw water balloons when you were a kid?"

"Yep."

"Do you feel that caused you to become an exceptionally violent adult?"

He smiled. "Not exceptionally, no."

She squinted at him, "You looked pretty…intense…about cornering those third-graders before."

"I was trying to teach them about courage under fire. It was a moral lesson."

"Like bible study."

"Exactly."

As easy at that, they were back on a friendly footing. Sarah knew how to handle people, he'd noticed. She was able to say the right thing, to put everyone at ease. When she wanted to, that was.

"Sure you don't want to stay?"

He wasn't sure, not by a long shot. Which made it even more imperative that he go. "I better not."

"Because you're afraid we're violent?" she asked.

"Because. Because of a lot of things. But not that." He hesitated. "There's a lot going on right now and it's complicated."

"Oh."

His answer seemed to make her shrink. He hadn't meant to make her feel bad, but they couldn't afford to kid themselves about the truth. He worked for her ex-husband, and so there couldn't be anything going on between them. End of story.

She fiddled with the hose, flipping the end to make the drops scatter on the driveway around her. "Charlie?" she said, her voice hesitant.

"Yep?"

"Do you... Did you notice... Does Simon seem normal to you? You were a boy and I never was and it's hard to guess..."

She was stammering so much it was painful, and Charlie, who didn't like to watch sitcoms because the action was too embarrassing, was surprised he wasn't recoiling. Instead, he wanted to reach out to her, pull her into his arms and stroke her hair, her back, until she'd calmed down enough to say whatever was so difficult for her.

But Sarah was off-limits. She had to be. So he did what he could, as a friend.

"Simon's all right." That sounded inadequate. "He'll find his way."

She shrugged one shoulder but didn't look up. If she did look up and she was crying, he was going to have to hold her. He'd never in his life wished for a woman to be crying.

"It's just that I wish his way was more like everybody else's. That would be easier."

"Easier's not always better."

"Mom, come here!" Simon yelled. She looked up at that but she wasn't crying. She smiled.

"Thanks for staying, Charlie. Thanks for…just… thanks."

He watched them in his rearview mirror long enough that it got uncomfortably warm in his car. A car coming toward him beeped, and he lifted a hand when he recognized Malcolm, the partner who'd pushed him into helping Sarah that first day. But when Malcolm stopped in front of Sarah's, and Lily climbed out of the backseat, Charlie started his car and got on his way. No sense inviting speculation when he wasn't even staying for pizza.

"Sorry I'm missing Vegas again," JT said.

"No big deal," Charlie answered. He was sitting on the top step of JT's back deck, shucking the corn he'd brought into a paper bag between his knees. He dropped the ear he'd just finished onto the platter.

JT squinted at the grill through a haze of smoke. There must have been too much marinade on the chicken he was cooking. Charlie chuckled when his brother coughed and backed away, fanning the air, as another cloud of smoke billowed up.

"At least last year we got to go to NASA," JT said. "That zero gravity simulator, remember? People dream all their lives about doing that, but because they don't have awesome big brothers with space connections, they die with their dream unfulfilled."

JT's company had won a contract to build a robotic telescope mount for the next Mars landing. The trip to NASA had been the culmination of years of work.

"NASA was your dream, JT. I wouldn't have died unhappy if I'd missed the chance to watch you do back-flips in zero gravity." Charlie picked up another ear of corn and ripped the husk off. This was the second year in a row JT was skipping the annual McNulty brothers Vegas pilgrimage to celebrate Charlie's birthday. Which wasn't a problem. He was turning thirty-two, not ten, after all. But he didn't need JT trying to make him feel better about it. In fact, he wished they could just stop talking about it.

"Hailey had a good idea. She said we can do a Vegas night here. It'll be Vegas except we'll be in Statlerville close to the hospital in case she has to go."

"Come on, JT," Charlie said. "Vegas night? At home? Sounds like a PTA fundraiser. Or a Sweet Sixteen party. No thanks. I'm fine, seriously."

He put the ear of corn on the platter and dug the last one out of the bag.

"Why not?"

"Can we just drop it?"

"I feel bad," JT said. "Why don't you go without me?"

"Because a single guy going to Vegas to celebrate his birthday alone is creepy."

"Why couldn't you find someone to go with you?"

"Why do you care so much about me and Vegas?" He finished the corn and rolled the top of the bag down to close it neatly. He took it around the corner of the house and dropped it into the garbage can before taking the corn platter back up on the deck. JT had retreated away from the smoke and was sitting on the end of a lounge chair flipping his tongs and catching them one-handed.

"I care," JT said, "because it's the only vacation you take all year. If I hadn't forced you to go to NASA last year, you'd have worked three hundred and sixty-five days in a row."

"I take weekends off," Charlie mumbled.

"You take Christmas off. And maybe a couple of Sundays in July," JT corrected.

Charlie grabbed the tongs in midair and advanced on the grill. "Who is all this food for, anyway?"

"Sarah and her kids are coming."

And that wouldn't be uncomfortable at all.

Charlie flipped the chicken and wished he'd stayed at home.

"I wish you'd told me that."

"Why?"

"It's awkward. I'm on the board at the school, and her kids have been suspended. The Ryan account... There's a lot of—"

He was reaching for a word when JT suggested, "Mess?"

"Exactly."

"Drama? Chaos? *Feelings?*"

"Shut up."

"You hate every second of it."

"Not as much as I hate you."

"Well, if you want to eat, you're going to have to cope."

Which was exactly what he didn't want to do. He didn't want to get to know Sarah any better or learn anything else he found irresistible about her. He didn't know how much more he could take.

He should look into cooking lessons. After the baby came no one here was going to be cooking very much, anyway, so he might as well learn to care for himself.

SARAH GRABBED HAILEY'S ARM and pulled her into the small pantry off the kitchen. The older farmhouse JT and Hailey bought after their wedding was full of nooks and old-fashioned spaces, like the butler's pantry that doubled as a walk-through from the kitchen to the dining room. "You didn't tell me Charlie was going to be here."

"I didn't know. He shows up a couple of times a week." Hailey took a sip from her rocks glass full of a pale green liquid. "He's cute. He always brings something with him, like he has to pay his way. I love a man with manners."

Sarah peered around the edge of the door. Charlie was sitting on the deck railing, one long leg resting on the lid of the cooler under him, the other swinging free. He was wearing navy pants and a forest-green polo shirt. His dark blond hair, cut short and neat, glistened in the sun. He lifted a bottle of beer and took a long swallow, his throat working in a way that was disturbingly sexy.

He was just drinking—how could that be sexy? Probably the same way throwing water balloons was sexy, not to mention that dance in the back of Wilton's.

She pulled her head back into the pantry and, picking up a can of diced pineapple, rubbed it on her forehead. It wasn't cold enough to do any good.

"Is that a margarita?" she said to Hailey. "Since when do you drink when you're pregnant?"

"Sarah?" Hailey said. "Is something wrong?"

"Hot flash."

"You're a little young for menopause."

"It's not menopause. I think it's Charlie."

"Charlie?" Hailey looked surprised. "Charlie, my brother-in-law Charlie?"

"Shush." Sarah tugged her sleeve. "Let me have a sip of that."

"Are you telling me you like Charlie McNulty?" She didn't give up the glass.

"Yes. No. I don't know. He's hot. I'm lonely. It's probably nothing more than that." Except she'd kept his reassurances about Simon in her mind as a buffer against her worries. That was more than just hormones. She pointed to the glass. "Are you going to share? Is there a pitcher somewhere?"

Hailey held her drink out of the way as she grabbed the can of pineapple from Sarah and put it back on the shelf. "But, Charlie?"

Sarah narrowed her eyes, thirsty for a margarita and impatient with Hailey's tone. "What does that mean?"

"Nothing. Just, you know. Brothers-in-law—they're… invisible…as men. Off-limits."

Sarah closed her eyes and thought about Charlie and the way he'd looked yesterday with his T-shirt clinging to his chest and shoulders. "Believe me, Hailey. He is not invisible. Not at all."

"Did this all happen because of Wilton's? Is it because he danced with you?"

"I've seen him a few other times." She managed to grab Hailey's glass and took a sip. She choked. "What is that? Is that even alcohol?"

"Pickle juice," Hailey said. She blushed. "Don't tell Olivia. She says I'm disgusting."

Sarah handed the glass back. "She's right."

"Getting back to you, isn't this is a little soon? And maybe a little close to home?"

Close to home? "Because of you and JT?"

"Because of Erik, Sarah. He works with Erik. You don't think this is because he's familiar and maybe, comfortable? What you're used to?"

Sarah peeked around the doorway again. Charlie was leaning on the deck railing, laughing at something the kids were doing in the yard. "Charlie is not what I'm used to, I promise you that."

"Well." Hailey drank another sip from her glass and then put it on the shelf. She pressed her hands at the small of her back and stretched. Her belly bumped the shelf across from her and a bag of angel hair pasta fell off. Sarah caught it before it hit the ground. "Just so you understand what you're up against, he's up for a promotion this year. A promotion Erik will have a say in. I don't see Charlie putting anything ahead of his career. He's just not that emotional."

"Who said anything about emotional?" Sarah asked. She might have emotional thoughts, but she definitely hadn't said them out loud. "The past couple of days made me realize something, Hailey. I'm sick of doing what I'm supposed to do. I've spent my whole life trying to measure up, and by all outside accounts, I've failed. My husband left me, my kids are criminals, the neighbors won't let their children come over, I'm not even allowed to serve the teachers their special lunch because I might taint their experience. Why should I try anymore? So I'm not. From now on, I'm doing what I want to do because it feels good."

"Whoa," Hailey said. "Sarah, where is this coming from?"

"From me. Finally, it's coming from me."

LILY SHRIEKED. SARAH TURNED her head to locate the kids in the yard. Olivia was playing soccer with them, and from the looks of things Lily had just scored a goal. She relaxed back into the cushions of the chaise. She wondered how JT and Hailey would feel about letting her and the kids move in. They could have a commune, sharing the responsibilities, and every night dinner would be just like this—good friends enjoying themselves together.

She was opening her mouth to ask Hailey if she could move in when JT said, "Charlie says Vegas night sounds like a fundraiser. He doesn't want to do it."

"JT!" Charlie exclaimed.

"What? You said it."

"That's okay," Hailey said. "I understand."

"What are you talking about?" Sarah asked.

Hailey, JT and Charlie all spoke at once.

"Charlie's birthday."

"Why my brother is such a loser."

"Nothing."

"Oh." Sarah rolled her eyes. "That was perfectly clear."

"JT and Charlie go to Vegas every year for Charlie's birthday," Hailey explained. "But they can't go this year because of the baby. So I suggested that we could do a Vegas night here." Hailey patted Charlie's leg. "But you can absolutely do the real thing in a few months. I'll be ready to have a break from JT by Christmas, I'm sure."

"Don't worry about it, Hailey," Charlie said. "Really."

"I never would have pegged you for the Vegas birthday type," Sarah said.

JT smacked his hand on the arm of his chair. "It's not what you're imagining, trust me. We go, he plays cards, wins a pile of money and then we come home."

"You win every year?" Sarah asked skeptically. "Erik lost five thousand dollars gambling when we were out there for our anniversary. He'd have lost more if we hadn't had to get on the plane to come home."

JT laughed. "Charlie doesn't exactly gamble. He only plays poker and he doesn't lose."

"That's impossible."

"Not for him," JT said. "It's more like watching a graduate-level math class than a Vegas vacation."

Charlie started grabbing plates off the table to pile on a tray to carry inside. "I'm sorry if I didn't memorize the *How to Act Like a Bozo in Vegas* handbook."

"But you don't do anything else? No slots?" Sarah asked. "No shows?"

"We went to see those guys with the tigers one time," JT said. He took a sip of his beer and showed no inclination to help his brother with the dishes. "But you were still in college—what was that, the year you turned twenty-one?"

Hailey started to get up to help Charlie clear up, but Sarah motioned for her to relax. "You rest. I need to hear more about the twenty-first-birthday tiger show."

Charlie groaned, but he held the screen door open for her as she carried a second tray of dirty dishes inside.

"So, about those tigers…" Sarah said, but then laughed at his aggrieved expression. "Kidding. You don't have to tell me."

"Siblings are a curse, aren't they?"

"Only child, here." She opened the dishwasher to start loading the glasses. "I was robbed of the sibling experience."

"You didn't miss anything. Nothing good, anyway."

Sarah wasn't sure she agreed with him on that count. She'd frequently wished for a sibling to absorb some of her parents' scrutiny. Her experiences with Simon and Lily were making her think that some of the flaws her parents had identified in her might have slipped under the radar if there'd been another kid or two on the scene. It was hard to worry obsessively over two children, and although she was giving it her all, she was sure she missed things. The knife for one. She'd missed that.

"I never had anybody to go to Vegas with," Sarah said. "So maybe *you* should count *your* blessings."

"I guess you've got me there."

"I'll tell JT you said so."

"Don't you dare."

He leaned down to put a stack of plates in the dishwasher and his arm brushed hers. She jerked back, jarring him, and he almost dropped the plates on the floor. "Sorry," she said.

"You okay?" he asked, his eyes meeting hers.

No, not really.

"Fine."

And also increasingly infatuated with Charlie McNulty, cardsharp, aggrieved little brother, sexy brother-in-law. Employee dependent on the good wishes of my ex-husband and his new wife.

She handed him another stack of plates and watched as he carefully fit them in the dishwasher, making sure they all faced the center. As an experiment, she grabbed a serving bowl from the counter and shoved it into the middle of the plate rack. He lifted it and turned it so it fit more neatly in the back.

Not exactly a "fling" kind of guy. Charlie was deliberate. Focused. Neat. Polite. Anal about the dishwasher. And all Sarah could think about was getting him alone somewhere and getting him naked.

SARAH AND HAILEY TOOK the kids to the country club to swim the following Tuesday. Because school was still in session and there were no other country club members with children who'd been suspended, Lily and Simon had the place and the lifeguard to themselves. The kids were doing pretty well playing together, so

Hailey and Sarah were lying on chairs under an umbrella, sharing a plate of French fries and a pitcher of lemonade.

"Where are the organic snacks?" Hailey asked. "Those tiny containers of peeled vegetables you always bring?"

"Welcome to my new lifestyle. I live for pleasure." She patted her stomach. She was wearing her lemon-yellow bikini that Erik had told her last summer she was getting too old to wear. She'd decided that this year she would wear nothing else.

"Not that I'm complaining or anything, because these French fries taste like heaven, but I'm concerned you might have some lime-Slurpee-colored vomit in your future. I couldn't believe Simon drank the whole thing."

"It's not right for a person to live six whole years without having tasted a Slurpee. I'm just happy I was able to provide him with that essential life experience." She looked fondly over at the pool where Lily was trying to teach Simon how to do a handstand. "You should have seen them devouring the Kraft macaroni and cheese. Simon was nervous about the color, but when he was finished he suggested we eat more orange foods."

"You're making me hungry." Hailey, her stomach covered by her red maternity suit, groaned and struggled upright. Even though she had her chair reclined and an extra pillow stuffed under her back, she wasn't able to get comfortable. "I still feel bad about Charlie's birthday," she said as she punched at the pillow. Sarah rolled up a towel and tucked it behind her in the chair.

"That better?"

Hailey grunted and sat back. She closed her eyes.

"Much. Thanks. Pregnancy is really badly designed, isn't it?" She squirmed until her hips settled comfortably on the towel. "Did he say anything to you the other night?"

"Not really."

"I have half a mind to just organize the Vegas night without asking him."

Sarah sat up. She wanted to see Charlie again and all the possibilities inherent in a fake Vegas night were exciting. "Let's do it."

The carriage house in Sarah's backyard where Hailey had lived before marrying JT was still without a tenant, so Sarah suggested they have the party there.

"Who are we inviting?" she said.

Hailey hesitated. "I don't know. I mean, if we do a big party that will be more fun for us, but Charlie would hate it."

"So what would he like?"

"I don't think he's going to like any of this."

"All right, then, we'll keep it small, and that way he can blow it off if he's not happy."

And if it was really small, it would give her more chances to convince him that he wanted to end his birthday party in her bed. Living for pleasure was sounding better and better every minute.

Sarah might not be allowed to serve strawberry short-cake at this year's teacher appreciation luncheon, but she'd been the perennial Tip Top PTA Volunteer award winner. She knew exactly how to organize a glitzy, Las Vegas–style fundraiser or a birthday party that looked just like a fundraiser, and more than that, she knew how to do it fast. Thank God for iPhones, she thought. From their chairs next to the pool, using a combination of Internet and cell-phone contacts, in less than two hours, they had planned Charlie's Vegas-night birthday party.

CHAPTER SEVEN

CHARLIE CLICKED THE REMOTE to turn off the iPod he kept in a docking station in his bedroom. He couldn't believe he was doing this. JT had told him about the party as soon as he found out Hailey and Sarah had planned it. They had intended to make it a surprise, but his brother knew there wasn't much he hated more than a surprise, and this party had a definite whiff of "over-the-top" before it had even gotten started.

On the way out of the bedroom, he flicked off the lights. The late-spring evening air filtering in from the street through the screen carried the sounds of the kids down the block playing tag. He really should stay home. He should have told them no.

He patted his pockets, checking for his wallet and cell phone, and then picked up his keys. His cell phone had started buzzing about two hours ago. JT. He guessed his brother was checking to be sure he wasn't going to blow them off. Since he didn't want to think too hard about why he was going, he'd switched the phone off.

Why was he going?

For Hailey. She and Olivia were the best things that had ever happened to his family and he wouldn't hurt her for the world. He knew Hailey felt bad about Vegas and he didn't want to make her feel worse.

And then there was Sarah. He couldn't get her out of his mind. She wasn't who he'd thought she was. And she sure as heck wasn't anyone he'd have thought he'd be interested in. Even aside from the fact that he knew he couldn't get involved with Erik's ex-wife and still expect the man to hand him a partnership, he found her challenging. He…well…when he was with her, he found it harder and harder to keep his self-control. The obvious solution was to avoid her. But there was something about her. Some spark. He liked being around her. He was scared of who he was when they were together, but he couldn't stop going back for more.

And besides, he couldn't not go. Sarah had been embarrassed enough recently. He wasn't about to shun her like Tina and her friend had done in the driveway after the water balloon fight.

He didn't want this party, but Sarah and Hailey wanted to give it for him, so that was that.

He'd dated a few women over the years. He had a definite type—tall, cultured, professional—the kind he'd figured out would be the perfect match to his own personality and the life he had planned. None of the relationships he'd had with his ideal women had worked out yet, but if he kept refining his search he'd eventually hit on the right person.

There wasn't much overlap between his type and short, snappy, sparky, unpredictable Sarah Finley. He was looking forward to seeing her.

Even if it was going to be at this Not-in-Vegas, Vegas birthday party.

HE PULLED THE MERCEDES around behind Sarah's house, fully expecting to see JT's MG there before him, but the driveway was empty. No sight of even Sarah's SUV. The carriage house was lit up like… well…like Vegas, though, so he headed over there. Christmas lights outlined the front porch and every window. A disco ball revolved slowly from the overhead fixture, and a strobe light flashed on the lawn highlighting a sign that read Vegas This Way. Tigers Enter in Back.

Funny.

He knocked but no one answered. Poking his head inside, he was surprised to see a roulette wheel and a poker table set up in the front room along with a full bar and a buffet table packed with food.

"Sarah!" he called, but there was no response.

He went back to Sarah's house and knocked on the patio door. Again, nothing but silence from the dark house.

He sat in one of the patio chairs and pulled out his phone. When he turned it on, he saw that there were seventeen new messages. All of them were from JT.

The pieces started to click into place, and he'd begun to figure out that he should have answered the phone when Sarah pulled in. He slid the phone into his pocket and walked across the patio to meet her.

"Where have you been?" she asked through the open window of her car.

"Hailey's in labor, isn't she?"

"She went to the hospital about an hour ago. They've been trying to call you since her labor started."

He held up his phone. "I turned it off. I thought JT was trying to make sure I didn't skip the party."

Sarah opened the door of her truck and swung her legs around to climb out. Charlie felt like someone had smacked him in the back of the head. Sarah was…Sarah was not looking much like Sarah usually looked.

She was wearing a very short skirt, for starters. A skirt so short and made of some kind of skinny, stretchy fabric that he wasn't sure should even be legal on the street. Where had she even bought something like that? he wondered stupidly. Did she have it shipped from Vegas? Because he was one hundred percent positive she hadn't found that thing in Statlerville.

She closed the door of the truck. Her midnight-blue shirt was clingy in all the ways a woman's shirt should be clingy, and Sarah had everything underneath that a woman should have. He remembered watching her on the sidelines at football games back in high school—the coach had benched him for three plays once to get him to concentrate on the game, but he'd spent the entire time watching Sarah bounce her way through a very interesting set of cheers. The coach had sent him back in disgust.

Where the hell had Sarah Finley found that outfit and why the hell hadn't she worn it sooner?

With an effort, he refocused. "I…I should call my brother."

"You can't call him now, Charlie," Sarah said. "His wife's in labor. He needs to be with her, not in the hall talking to you."

"Oh. Right." He rubbed his temples. He felt disoriented. "I've never become an uncle before. At least not while the kid was still a baby."

Charlie hadn't met Olivia until two years ago, when she was fifteen and JT and Hailey got together.

Sarah pressed the button on her key chain to lock her car and then faced him. "I just got back from their house. I took my kids over so Olivia could watch them during the party. They were supposed to be having a sleepover with her." She gestured over her shoulder, and the silky shirt slid sideways enough to give him a hint that she was possibly wearing a black bra. He wouldn't have thought Sarah was a black-bra kind of person. He wondered how hard it would be to get a better look so he'd know for sure. "Anyway, Hailey had to go right after we got there, but I talked to JT once she got checked in and they're fine."

Charlie nodded, not really taking in what she said except for the part where Hailey was doing okay. "So where are your kids? And Olivia?"

"Your dad is there with the kids. Olivia is going to go to the hospital for a while, but she doesn't want to stay. I think she's grossed out by the whole thing, so your dad will spend the night with all of them. Hailey and JT had it all arranged weeks ago for him to watch Olivia, and he said he didn't mind if my guys hung around, too."

Charlie shook his head. "The new Jack McNulty, doting grandpa, is never going to seem natural to me."

Two years ago, when his mother died and JT came back to town, their family had changed in ways he was still learning to trust. His dad had been injured in an accident but was back to most of his usual activities thanks to Hailey's work on his physical therapy and JT's care. Jack was more connected to the family, and his relationship with Olivia was remarkable to his sons, who'd grown up intimidated by their volatile dad. Jack would never actually be mellow, but he was infinitely more human. While Charlie certainly enjoyed the new-formula Dad, he wasn't as comfortable with him as JT was.

"He's good with the kids."

"So, what…um. What are you going to do?" Charlie asked.

He tried to keep his voice neutral, but either he failed or Sarah's mind was on the same wavelength as his, because she smoothed her hands down the sides of her skirt, molding it to her sweet curvy hips, and said, "Want to go to Vegas?"

CHAPTER EIGHT

IT SHOULD HAVE BEEN awkward, and maybe there was a second, right when they walked in the door of the carriage house and it was just the two of them, that it was. But it didn't take long for them to start having fun. Charlie was excellent company.

Right.

Charlie was superhot. She was wearing an outfit that made her feel like someone else. He kept trying to peek down her shirt and she kept trying to let him. That all added up to a surefire party-starter combination in her opinion.

She needed to thank Hailey later for telling her to upgrade her underwear collection before she tried to seduce anyone. She'd said men liked it if you made the pursuit worthwhile and JT had walked in at that moment. Hailey had given him a scorching kiss, which made Sarah figure her friend knew what she was talking about.

So she was wearing a black bra under her sexy outfit. The kind of bra that lifted and assisted in the right ways. Or at least the saleswoman's assurances that it lifted and assisted in the right ways seemed to be true. If Charlie tried any harder to pretend he wasn't staring at her chest, he might pull something.

Boys.

She hadn't had this much fun in years. Maybe ever. When she'd been single and dating she'd always felt so awkward. Her mom had thought putting her in beauty pageants would give her poise and self-confidence, but all it had really done was confirm that while she was cute enough, her real strength was her personality, so she needed to work extra hard to be sure people liked her.

Having Hailey Maddox, the kind of beautiful girl who was meant to be prom queen, as her best friend hadn't done much to boost her confidence, either. It was a given that in any situation, Sarah was going to be the best friend. The bubbly best friend. Who almost always was pretty enough to date the cute guy's best friend. But who never got the cute boy himself.

Erik hadn't even picked her first. She'd met him at the Pan-Hellenic formal her junior year at Villanova. She'd gone stag with a bunch of her sisters from Delta Gamma while he'd been with a senior from the Chi Omega house. His date had ditched him halfway through dinner, and he'd been in the lobby trying to call a taxi when Sarah and her sisters met him. He'd looked so dejected that she'd asked him if he wanted to come with them. They'd wound up making out in the back of a cab on the way to a bar, but then he'd spent the rest of the night coming on to one of the other juniors from her house.

They'd spent most of the next two years hooking up at parties when he was in between girlfriends. Every time he started dating someone else, Sarah swore she wouldn't take him back, but somehow she always did. He'd finally settled down with Casey Hall, a gorgeous girl from Long Island who played tennis for the varsity team and double-majored in French and business. He proposed to Casey at the end of senior year, but she turned him down. And then he and Sarah both wound up in New York City after school—she was waitressing and Erik had an internship on Wall Street. They dated and he asked her to marry him at Christmas. Looking back, she wasn't even sure why she'd said yes.

She definitely couldn't remember ever being so turned on by Erik, and Charlie hadn't done a thing yet besides look at her.

Please let him be working up to doing something more.

They'd started with roulette—and a gin and tonic for her, a Scotch for him. He'd bet methodically even though the game was just for fun and he'd walked away with a large pile of chips.

"Want another drink?" he asked from behind the bar.

"I should eat if I'm having another one," she said.

He poured more Scotch into his glass and brought her drink to her. "What's on the menu?"

"Hailey brought M&M's," she said.

"You left the food up to Hailey?"

"I left the M&M's up to Hailey."

She'd gone overboard with the food planning, but she figured with her new outcast status she wasn't going to be entertaining anytime soon. And besides, she liked food. And she'd wanted Charlie to be happy.

Mission accomplished, she concluded as Charlie put another jumbo shrimp on his plate and she grabbed a second miniature Reuben from the warming dish. Piling plates high, they sat at the small round table near the buffet. When they'd finished their dinner and returned with plates of dessert—chocolate-covered fruit and slices of cheesecake—Sarah said, "Good party."

Charlie nodded, his mouth too full to answer.

"What's the deal with Vegas? You count cards?"

Charlie shrugged. "Poker's partly chance but mostly knowing the percentages. I understand it."

"But why do you have to go to Vegas? Couldn't you get a poker game in New York City?"

"No, that's illegal. Foxwoods in Connecticut, maybe." He shrugged again. "Vegas is tradition, I guess." But he was concentrating a little too hard on his cheesecake. It was good, but not that good. She pushed.

"JT said you like to tempt yourself—like a test of will. Get surrounded by all that occasion of sin and then walk away clean as a whistle."

"And that would be why he's an engineer, not a therapist. No people skills."

Sarah smiled. "I'm a mother, Charlie. I recognize misdirection. If it's not a test of moral strength, why, then?"

"Potential," he said so softly she almost didn't hear him. *Potential?*

Sarah leaned over the table, her fork poised above a blueberry that had fallen off his cheesecake. "May I?"

She didn't like blueberries, but the leaning gave her a chance to flash her cleavage again. She didn't normally have cleavage, but the bra was doing a wonderful job. She was turned on a little by her own cleavage and she wasn't even a guy.

Charlie pushed his plate forward with two fingers, and she made sure to raise the fork with the berry extra slowly to her mouth. His eyes followed the movement, and she caressed the fork with her lips in a way she'd only ever seen in the movies. She wasn't even sure she was doing it right and had almost decided she looked like a fool when she saw him shift in his seat as if he was suddenly uncomfortable. He hadn't taken his eyes off her mouth. So, yeah, it looked like she was doing it right. *God, did she love Vegas.*

"Potential what?" she asked. "Money?"

He rested his fork on the edge of his plate and then pushed it the rest of the way into the middle of the table. He hitched his chair closer to hers. "You ever go out there, Sarah?"

"Just once, with Erik."

"When you're there, it's like you could be anybody. There are so many people and so many things. You could literally be anything, probably do anything. That's why I like it."

"But you play poker and then you come home," she said. "You don't do anything."

"But I might."

HE MIGHT. HE MIGHT KISS SARAH. He might feed her blueberries. He might get to see that bra up close and personal, and then he might get to see the rest of her. What the hell was happening right here in Statlerville, Pennsylvania?

Charlie had never told anyone what he liked about Vegas. He and JT had been flying out there for fourteen years, ever since he'd turned eighteen, and he'd never even told his brother.

This night felt different to him, though. It was just him and Sarah, and who'd ever have thought they'd be spending time together?

She didn't look like herself, she'd done something to her hair so it was both more controlled and more outrageous than usual. And her shirt and that little skirt and her heels and the subtle scent he caught every time he leaned over her. She wasn't acting like herself, either. He had no idea why it was so sexy, but that thing she'd done with her mouth and the fork and the berry had shot straight through him. He was turned on by fruit. And cutlery.

No. He was turned on by Sarah.

Night had fallen and the two of them were closed up in the little house, and they wouldn't be disturbed until morning. It was all so private. He imagined he could say things to Sarah and it wouldn't matter later. She wanted this and he wanted to see what it felt like to be with someone when he hadn't planned every detail.

He'd always known he had some of his mother inside him. His whole life, every time he planned to take it easy, hang back, he'd found himself tripped up by his ambition or his pride and he'd push to the front row. It had happened as far back as high school when he'd decided to go out for defense but somehow had found himself on the line with the other quarterback hopefuls.

And now here he was with Sarah. Sweet, sexy Sarah. Just the two of them. Alone.

"You know that saying, 'What happens in Vegas stays in Vegas'?" she asked.

He nodded, his pulse racing.

"There's a sign outside that says this is Vegas, right?"

He nodded again. She licked her lips. She had a great mouth, a wide smile and lips with a generous curve just like the one in her hips.

"I've never played poker, but it's your birthday so we should, right?"

"Whatever you want, Sarah."

"No," she said softly. "This is your party. It's what you want."

"Okay. Poker is good."

She leaned over and put her hand on his thigh. "Strip poker?"

His leg jerked and he hit his knee on the table. Her hand got caught in between.

She pulled her hand back and shook it out, laughing.

"Oh, God, I'm sorry, Sarah."

She threw her head back, exposing the slender column of her pale throat, and for that second she was the Sarah he thought he knew, funny, engaging, ordinary Sarah Finley, except he couldn't see her that way anymore. She was more now that he'd seen this sexy, edgy side of her, and he had to clutch the sides of his chair to keep from reaching for her.

"Something funny?" he asked. He hadn't expected her to laugh.

"It's just…I was nervous. I didn't know if you'd think that was a weird thing to say." She gave her hand a last shake. "But I'm guessing you're interested."

She might be laughing, but he was not wrong about the way she was looking at him. She'd asked him to play strip poker and she wanted him to say yes. He was not wrong that Sarah Finley was ready to be seduced and that he was the man to do it.

He got up and stood over her. Then he put his hands on the arms of her chair and leaned down. He made sure to get close enough that his breath stirred a curl just behind her ear. He felt her legs move apart, and he brought his own leg up in between them, pressing against one of hers so the warmth of her bare calf heated him through his pants. "I think strip poker is an excellent plan. Because you see, Sarah," he whispered before he pulled back so he could see her eyes, "anticipation is half the fun."

She let out a soft sigh and caught her bottom lip in her teeth, and he squeezed the arms of the chair tighter. He wasn't going to touch her, not yet. But he wanted to. More every second. "Also?" he whispered. "I never lose."

"Oh," she breathed. "We'll see about that."

He bent his knee so he was practically kneeling over her and pressed his lips to the sensitive skin under her ear. "Get the cards, sweetheart," he whispered. "But remember I warned you. I'm very good with numbers."

SHE WON THE FIRST HAND, but only because she'd planned ahead and tucked a spare ace under her plate. She pulled it out when he wasn't looking and added it to her hand. She thought he'd seen, but he didn't say anything so she played on. She really wanted him to take off some of his clothes, but the idea of taking off her own was almost as exciting. She'd never done anything like this. She'd had trouble breathing when she suggested it because she worried that he'd say no. Or that it would be awkward. But it wasn't. What was a word that meant "deliciously exciting" and also "sexually charged"? That was the word she needed to describe strip poker with Charlie.

He took off his shoes and kicked them back under his chair. She wondered if finding brown dress socks sexy was a symptom of some kind of sexual disorder. She could worry about that tomorrow. In the meantime, Charlie was dealing and he was still wearing pants, which meant she had work to do.

When he won the next hand and she reached down, he put his hand on hers, cupping the heel of her shoe, holding it in place. "You should leave those on."

"But you took your shoes off," she protested. She hadn't really thought about what to take off first—she'd just been following his lead.

He ran his hand up the back of her calf, his eyes following the progress. He skimmed his fingers across the hollow at the back of her knee and then sat back. His voice was rough when he said, "My shoes were in the way. Yours could be…fun."

Fun? For what? If she left them on, when would she take them off? She didn't want to be sitting around in nothing but her underwear and high heels.

Oh.

Good point.

Charlie clearly had a better handle on the potential found in women's clothing than she did. She wished she was better at this but she'd never done it before. Never tried to seduce someone. She'd always felt so…insignificant. She'd figured seduction was best done by women who were sexier. But Charlie. He was making this easy. She lost her heart to him a little bit right there. Right when he told her to keep her shoes on because it might be fun.

She considered for a moment and then lifted her arm and shook her gold-link bracelet down to her wrist. She took her time wiggling and sliding it over her knuckles and off the tips of her fingers. She let it slither through her cupped hands into a pile next to her cards.

Charlie growled and she got up to refill their drinks, partly because she was thirsty and partly to hide the idiotic grin that kept popping out during her seduction. It was a thrill to feel so powerfully sexy—she wouldn't ruin it by grinning.

When she got back to the table, he'd already dealt the next hand. "You're not allowed to deal when I'm not at the table," she said. Then she turned her cards over and saw a two, a three and a joker. As far as she knew the jokers had been taken out of the deck before they started playing. They were useless, right? She looked at him, but he was leaning back in his chair, his cards held in a lazy hand on his chest.

"Lodge a protest," he drawled. "Management's having a baby, but I bet she'll take your call."

Sarah thought about the way his lips had felt on her neck and the way he couldn't keep his eyes off her shirt. "This is fine," she said, fanning her cards demurely. "I'm sure you would never cheat me."

"Damn straight I wouldn't." He sipped his Scotch, and who would have guessed blue eyes could smolder? "Everything I do has your best interests at heart."

When she lost that hand, she took off her shirt. The black bra had such a good effect on her breasts and that in turn had such a good effect on Charlie that she thought she might just write the manufacturer a thank-you letter. Never in all her years had Sarah ever felt so desired. And he still hadn't even touched her. She kept her core straight and thanked the Lord for Pilates.

"Would you get me another piece of cheesecake?" she asked.

While Charlie was at the buffet, she dealt him the joker, a five and the queen of diamonds, and with four disastrous bets he'd lost all his chips. He hadn't taken his eyes off hers once as he played the hand. She didn't think he'd even glanced at the cards she gave him, so it didn't matter that she'd slipped him another joker and a two from the stack next to her glass.

"I lose," he said. She licked her lips.

Sarah raked in the pot, but she wasn't paying any attention to it. All of her focus was on Charlie, who had stood to unbutton his shirt. He wasn't exactly stripping, but he wasn't exactly not. He started at the top—long, lean fingers flicking each button open while his gaze stayed locked on hers. When the shirt was open, he turned away from her and shrugged it off, slowly revealing powerfully molded shoulders, a long, strong back and a waist that tapered smoothly.

When God made Charlie McNulty, he brought his A-game.

He sat down again, leaning back, his legs spread wide. She wanted to touch him so badly, but she wasn't ready for the game to end. The cards were piled haphazardly by her elbow, so she picked them up and stacked them neatly. His eyes flicked from her hands to her breasts to her face. She read hunger in them, but it was different from the sexual need she'd grown used to with Erik. Charlie wanted *her,* specifically her. She felt the connection with him every time she moved. He was turned on by her outfit and the night and the way she moved, and she loved it. She dropped a card under his chair and slid off her own to kneel down and get it. When she had it in her hand, she sat up straight on her knees, her breasts just touching him, the rough fabric of his jeans making her want to press forward.

"Sorry," she said. "I dropped a card." She met his eyes and flinched away from the heat in his expression. He moved his knees, lazily caressing her skin, aware of exactly what he was doing to her.

"Dropped card makes this a penalty round," he said.

She bit her lip, pretending to be scared. "Penalty? That sounds…dangerous."

"It means the loser has to take off what the winner demands."

She nodded, but he held up his hand. "No, wait. Rule change. It means the winner gets to take something off the loser."

He wanted to undress her.

Sarah reached backward and slid up onto her chair, never taking her eyes off his. She didn't know how this was possible, but he was amazing and he wanted her.

She dealt the cards and didn't even cheat this time. She couldn't decide if she wanted to win or lose, so she left it up to fate.

Fate must be a woman, she thought a few minutes later as Charlie stood and said, "Your choice."

She swallowed. He was tall and strong and he was standing in front of her, arms slightly raised from his sides, ready to submit to her. The low lights turned his skin a beautiful gold; the shadows in his shoulders and chest where his muscles deepened were mesmerizing. She could do what she wanted with him. To him. He wanted her to choose.

She stood slowly, pressing her skirt down over her hips just because she wanted to make him sweat. She backed a few paces away from the table, then beckoned him forward until there were a few scant inches of space between them. She put her fingertips on his stomach, spreading her hands to feel the hard muscle, smoothing lightly over the trail of hair. He stood perfectly still, but his breath came faster.

She moved on to his belt, sliding the end of the leather back through the buckle, tugging to lift the latch and pressing her hand against him as she worked it free. He moved then, pushing back against her, and she could feel the heat of him through his jeans.

"Sarah," he breathed out, his voice cracking. "You're killing me."

"It's a penalty round," she said primly. "It's supposed to hurt."

She slid the belt out of the first loop, one hand flat on the front of his waist, the other guiding the belt, caressing his hips, the curve of his ass, teasing in the waistband of his boxers as she moved her arm around him. When she finally dragged the belt free from the last loop, she stayed pressed against him, her skin tingling where it touched his. She dropped the belt on the floor and, without looking away from him, swept her arm across the table, sending the cards and chips to the floor. "Oops. Las Vegas has suffered an earthquake."

"What happened to anticipation?" Charlie asked, pressing his hips into hers.

"Honestly?" Sarah whispered, her eyes on level with his chest. He nodded.

"You took off your shirt," she said.

The light dusting of hair on his chest was matched by the soft line that descended with tantalizing mystery down his stomach. His jeans, without the belt, hung low on his hips, leaving the band of his black boxers exposed. Sarah wrapped her hands around him again, pressing him against her, using the belt loops above either hip. He let himself be pulled until they were standing skin to skin again, her arms around his waist.

He leaned his forehead on hers. "You're sure about this, Sarah?"

If he ever lost his job, she thought, he could get hired in the phone sex industry in a heartbeat. The clear, mellow tones of his voice were made for whispering dirty suggestions on a 900 line.

"I'm sure," she said. Before she'd even finished speaking, he'd put his arms under her thighs and lifted her, pushing her skirt higher up her legs and making her pulse speed with the thrill of being held so powerfully. She let her body sink into his, and he took her weight without seeming to notice.

"You're sure?" he asked again as he kissed her neck and nibbled a path toward her ear.

"Yes," she managed to say between breaths. "Charlie, I want this. Please."

He didn't need any more encouragement. He let her slide down, not once removing his hands from her body, trailing them up her bare thighs as her skirt bunched up near her ass.

He caressed the bare skin of her back, her sides, the tops of her breasts. He ran his fingers under the cups of her bra, barely brushing her nipples, but she jerked forward with such intense sensation it startled her.

"I knew this was black," he murmured. "Saw it outside."

She arched her back, hoping to encourage him to take it off, but he spent a few more minutes playing with the edges, teasing until she couldn't stand it. What was he waiting for?

"Charlie!"

He looked up. "What?"

"Anticipation time is officially done."

He gave her a wicked grin and had her bra off and his hands on her breasts faster than it took her to think *jackpot!*

HE'D ALMOST STOPPED. He'd had her in his arms, her shirt off, her body almost more than he could stand. But as he was about to open her bra, he realized this was Sarah. He knew her and he didn't screw around with people he knew like this.

But then he remembered her Drunken Breakdown. This must be the next step. The Rebound Guy. He'd be her Rebound Guy. Give them both this one night here in this fake world. Tomorrow they'd go back to their normal lives and she'd be one step closer to healing and finding the guy she really wanted to be with.

He ignored the stab of envy when he thought about who that guy might be. Sarah was incredibly hot and they were both turned on. No reason they shouldn't both have something to remember.

Her breasts, like everything about her compact body, were on the small side, but they looked exactly right. Her beautiful pale skin flushed with desire.

He slid his hands down her sides to the waistband of her skirt. He loved the flare of her hips and ass. She wasn't built like a lingerie model, but there was more than enough of her to keep his hands and his eyes occupied. He plunged his hands down under the waist of the skirt and cupped her ass, pulling her closer to him. She came willingly and lifted her face.

Their kiss was hot, tongues and lips and breath all tangled up, driving him higher and harder than a kiss had ever done.

"Sarah," he breathed. "You're… You're… This—"

"Exactly," she said. "Me, too."

THEY KEPT KISSING, hot, deep kisses, and he kept moving his hands, stroking her back and her ass, rubbing her breasts, teasing her to impossible heights. She got her hands up between them and worked the button and zipper on his jeans. He moaned against her throat. She put her palm on him and felt him press against her.

She lost track of time then. She managed to push his

jeans down and he stepped back long enough to shuck them all the way off, his boxers following. She barely had time to take him in, a gorgeous, lean man, before he'd pulled her close again and her skirt was being peeled down her thighs. He took his time, teasing and stroking, and when she was finally naked, she wasn't sure how much more she could stand. They moved backward and wound up on the couch. He was too tall to fit comfortably lying down so he sat up and pulled her to straddle his lap.

Finally, when she couldn't take one more second, she stopped kissing him, licked her lips and tried to focus.

"Do you want to—"

"Yes," he said. "But I don't…"

She slipped off his lap and walked over to the bar. For one second she felt self-conscious in her heels and nothing else, but then she glanced over her shoulder and saw the way his eyes gleamed and she straightened up. Sarah, perennial runner-up, knew what the pageant winner's strut looked like. She reached into her purse, grabbing a condom from the packet she'd bought that afternoon, and then walked back to him, savoring his appreciation.

"You were right about the shoes," she said as she handed him the condom.

"You're telling me."

He pulled her back down and she took him inside, the stretch uncomfortable at first—it had been too long. But soon it was so good. She leaned back and let her mind empty as she and Charlie McNulty made love.

WHEN CHARLIE WOKE UP it was still dark. He was stretched uncomfortably on the couch, his legs hanging over the arm, Sarah lying on top of him. He'd thought he would spend the whole night, but now that he'd cooled off, he knew he should leave. Rebound guys were almost surely awkward breakfast companions. He ran a hand down Sarah's side, enjoying the smooth muscles of her waist and the flare of her hips blending into her thigh. She responded to his touch, nuzzling closer under his chin.

He'd loved everything about the night, and that, of course, was the problem. He couldn't be with Sarah, not this way. Even beyond the personal obstacles between them, he didn't want to be with someone like her, especially not doing things like they'd done last night. She'd made him lose control, seduced him into the kind of play and passion he didn't want to engage in, the parts of himself he tried hardest to suppress. They'd connected so totally he'd been surprised. It had been great for the one night. But that was all he wanted it to be.

He eased out from under her and dressed in the dark. Then he knelt next to the couch and brushed her hair back so he could kiss her forehead. "Sarah," he said softly. She stirred. "I have to go." Her eyes opened all the way and she reached for him.

"Don't go," she said sleepily. "We could still have morning sex."

A proposition he definitely wanted to take her up on, but he knew that would complicate the situation more than necessary. One ill-considered...session...was something he hoped they could get past. Any repeat performance would be too much.

"I'll see you, okay?"

She blinked, her eyes unfocused, her hair tousled, her lips…oh, damn.

Three, seven, twelve, no…thirteen.

Reciting prime numbers in his head should have been distracting enough, but he couldn't remember the next one. He noticed a throw blanket on the floor. They must have kicked it off. He stretched it over her and tucked it in near her feet.

"Sarah, this was great. Thanks," he muttered as he checked to be sure she'd stay warm when he was gone.

She blinked again, and he wasn't entirely sure she'd understood him. But he couldn't afford to linger. He had to get out and get his life back on track.

SARAH WOKE UP ALONE. For a moment she was completely confused. For one thing, she was naked. Fully covered by a blanket, but still, naked. She didn't sleep naked. Erik didn't like it and Simon sometimes wandered into her room… *Wait.* This wasn't her room. She sat up and looked frantically around.

The couch.

The carriage house.

Vegas night.

Charlie.

Where was Charlie?

She fell back onto the couch as the memory of him whispering to her in the night came back. He'd said he had to go. Had he said where? She couldn't remember.

However, her toes curled as she stretched. She did remember everything else. Clutching the blanket to her chest, Sarah picked her way through the remains of Vegas night and let herself out of the carriage house. She scampered across the driveway to her patio. The grass was wet with dew and the gravel sharp under her bare feet, but she didn't mind.

She didn't mind any of it. She relished the feel of the cool morning air where it tickled her bare skin under the blanket, reminding her of last night and how Charlie had looked as he touched her, making her feel like the most gorgeous woman in the world. She almost hoped one of her neighbors was awake and had seen her running naked across the yard. She wanted to share how alive she felt with the whole world.

CHAPTER NINE

"YOU ARE THE MOST PERFECT baby in the history of humans," Sarah said as she gently kissed Tyrel McNulty's forehead. He was securely swaddled from shoulders to toes in a flannel receiving blanket. A blue knit cap covered everything else down to the tips of his ears, but Sarah could tell, just from the expression on his sleeping face, that Tyrel was brilliant, funny and in all ways wonderful.

She'd stopped by the hospital early, congratulating JT and Olivia as they slipped out to get breakfast. JT had seemed shell-shocked, but proud and relieved his wife and baby were safe. Olivia already had Tyrel's picture on her phone and was talking about setting up a Web site so they could share pictures with JT's colleagues in the Pittsburgh office. Sarah could stay only a few minutes as she had to hurry to pick up the kids—Jack was eager to meet his grandson.

Hailey's tired smile indicated agreement even as she said, "I'm just glad he finally arrived. Me and pregnant are not a good mix."

Sarah turned away from the windows and carried the baby back to the bed. "Feeling more like yourself now?"

"Much," Hailey said.

Sarah nuzzled Tyrel's neck. "You were right about the baby smell. It's the best."

Hailey tilted her head to the left. "You're happy."

Sarah hummed to the baby.

"If I were still pregnant, this mood of yours would be irritating me. You're so happy, it's verging on obnoxious."

Sarah pulled Tyrel closer to her chest and rocked him gently. She kissed his nose. Tyrel was JT's middle name, and she thought he was lucky to be one of the McNulty men. Whatever their issues, they were a strong family.

"If I didn't know better, I'd think you'd... Wait a minute. Oh my God. You had sex with my brother-in-law, didn't you?" Hailey pulled her blanket up over her mouth. "I can't believe I just said that. You and Charlie?"

"Me and celibate are not a good mix," Sarah said. She took in a deeper breath of the delicious newborn scent and knew her smile had become stupidly silly.

"You. Did. Not." Hailey pointed at her. "Even when we talked about it, I never thought it would work. You actually seduced Charlie."

She laughed. She'd forgotten how good it felt to share a secret adventure with a girlfriend. It had been years since she'd done anything she would have been tempted to keep secret, even longer since she'd done anything that was worth sharing.

"Sarah!" Hailey said. "Tell me everything. Put the baby down first—he's too young to hear this."

Sarah sat in the burnt-orange padded chair next to the bed. "I can't tell you details," she said. "What happens in Vegas stays in Vegas."

"But…" Hailey sputtered. "This is Charlie. *Nothing* happens in Vegas. JT told me their trip is a huge bore. What do you mean things happened in Vegas and I can't hear about them?"

Sarah remembered how Charlie had acted last night—in control, loose, funny and so incredibly good at what he did. She loved seeing him like that, without his buttoned-up shell, and she especially loved the powerful feeling that she'd been the one to draw him out. She'd never in her life been the instigator of a sexual encounter. Last night, the way Charlie had looked at her as if he'd needed her, wouldn't be okay without her, well, it had been a heady experience.

"I guess I wasn't the only one who's been feeling sparks." Tyrel started to stir. She leaned over to hand him to Hailey. "Thanks for the tip about the underwear. Very good advice."

Hailey pulled the baby closer, folding the edge of the blanket back. "He's getting hungry," she murmured. Sarah stood.

"I have to pick up the kids. They're so mad I couldn't bring them. Lily's writing a letter of protest to the hospital. Something about you and I being blood sisters, which makes Tyrel her half cousin, which means they should be allowed on the maternity ward and not kept out like, as she put it, common strangers from the street. You don't think she's reading Sinclair during her suspension, do you?"

Hailey was busy arranging her gown and positioning her son, but she paused. "Sarah. Don't…I mean…I'm not even sure what I'm trying to say. I love Charlie. But he's, well, not exactly a guy who connects with people. I guess…don't expect too much from him. Not when that promotion thing is hanging over his head."

"No expectations," Sarah said. She smiled breezily, attempting to channel some independent, saucy persona. Mary Tyler Moore throwing her cap in the air. No worries. Everything was fine. "It was a fun night. That's all."

As she waited for the elevator, though, she hugged herself. It hadn't been just a fun night. It had been the best night. She and Charlie had really clicked and he'd finally seemed to stop expecting her to go crazy. He'd gone a little bit crazy himself. She knew, just knew, that he was going to want more.

CHARLIE SPLIT TOWN. He'd been too keyed up to sleep after coming home from Sarah's, so he'd spent the rest of the night in his study, going over the plans for Henry Ryan and mapping out a strategy for the meeting they had coming up that week. At first he'd had trouble concentrating—Sarah kept intruding on his thoughts—but he'd trained himself long ago to block out unproductive thoughts. Without a doubt, sexual fantasies about Sarah Finley were unproductive. By six-fifteen he was ready for a shower, his plans for Ryan complete, and Sarah was on her way to being a social acquaintance, a great memory, and nothing more.

A really great memory, he thought as he leaned his forehead against the shower wall, letting the hot water pound down on his neck and back. A freaking kick in the pants. She'd cheated him. *At strip poker.* She was amazing. He'd had no idea. He wondered what the hell

Erik Finley was doing with Lauren when he could have had Sarah. With his eyes still closed, he flipped the lever on the shower most of the way toward cold.

He needed to get out of here so he could get his perspective back. He called the airline and made a reservation. He'd go to Vegas for real and get his head straight. JT had said he needed a vacation, and obviously he'd been right. How else could he explain what he'd done with Sarah?

About an hour before he was supposed to leave, he was at the hospital to meet his new nephew. He knocked lightly on the open door, but no one heard him. JT was stretched out in the bed with Hailey, one leg on the floor, one hand stroking the hair away from her forehead. Charlie was about to go in when he saw his dad hold the baby up so he could look out the window toward downtown.

Charlie leaned on the doorjamb, his throat tight as he watched his dad.

"Half an hour, Tyrel, that's all it takes to get to the stadium." Jack tucked the baby back against his chest. "We're going in for a game just as soon as your mom's back is turned."

"He can't eat hot dogs until he has teeth," Hailey called.

"And no souvenir foam finger until he grows out of the choking years," JT added.

Olivia, standing at Jack's right shoulder, folded the blanket in tight around the baby's feet as she said, "My brother might like the Mets. Don't try to warp him before he's old enough to make an informed choice."

"The Mets will never be an informed choice," Jack

murmured, his face close to his grandson's. "No one with any taste likes the Mets."

"I like the Mets," Olivia protested.

Jack bumped Olivia's shoulder with his elbow. "Your only flaw, kid. Everyone's entitled to one."

Jack had been tough when he and JT were kids, probably harder for his brother than him because he and Jack had at least connected over sports. After his parents kicked JT out, Charlie hadn't been able to figure out how to get his stubborn family to bridge their differences. But Olivia had come along and somehow both Jack and JT were able to put aside their issues and they had learned to be a family again. In a way. Things were better. Good, even. It surprised him sometimes.

Hailey noticed Charlie and nudged her husband. "Your brother's here," she said quietly.

Charlie met JT halfway across the room and he pulled him into a hard hug. "Congratulations, man," Charlie said. "You guys deserve to be happy."

JT thumped him between the shoulder blades. "You do, too." Charlie remembered Sarah after they'd made love the first time last night. She'd been sitting on the back of the couch, tossing M&M's and trying to catch them in her mouth—she was laughing and beautiful.

He released JT and stepped back to grab the gift bag he'd left at the door.

Hailey kissed him as he handed the bag over. "Thanks, Charlie. Sorry we missed your birthday."

He was about to tell her not to worry about it when she added, "At least you and Sarah had fun."

And then she winked.

Damn.

She knew. Could be girlfriend ESP, but more than likely Sarah had been here earlier.

"Yeah," he muttered. "She throws a great party."

Hailey grinned.

Jack brought the baby over to him. "You want to hold your nephew?"

Charlie backed up a step, but Olivia was right behind him, blocking his way. "Uncle Charlie, he's not going to break."

"Unless you drop him on his soft spot," Hailey said, and even though he knew she was joking, he still tensed up.

"His soft what?"

But Jack had somehow maneuvered the baby into his arms and he was holding the blanket-wrapped form of the newest McNulty. Tyrel's eyes were closed, his tiny hands still where they curled on the edges of the blanket, but Charlie could feel how alive the baby was, right through the blanket. He shifted him a little higher and then looked up. JT's eyes locked on his.

"Amazing," Charlie said.

Olivia snapped a picture. When he looked back at the baby, she snapped another. "When you have your own kids," Olivia said, "you'll be a pro."

Hailey swung her legs out of the bed and pulled the ties on her flannel robe tighter. "Olivia, let's take Tyrel for a walk."

Charlie handed the baby over and said, "I'll head out with you."

"Dad and I wanted to talk to you for a second," JT said.

Hailey and Olivia were scurrying for the door without

a backward glance and he realized that JT and Jack had closed ranks behind them. He'd just been set up.

"What?" he said, not wanting to give them time to regroup.

"Dad wants to go with you to Vegas," JT said.

"Well, that's a nice idea and everything, but my flight leaves in two hours, and Dad's not packed, so I think he'll have to take a rain check."

Jack lifted a duffel bag out from behind the chair. "I'm packed."

"I didn't realize you had a Vegas trip planned, too," Charlie said, desperately stalling for time while he tried to figure out how to get out of this. He was leaving town to forget about Sarah, to straighten his head out. Being around his dad was never relaxing and, more than that, he had a bad feeling this whole setup had to do with the fact that Hailey, and probably JT, and more than likely Jack, all knew he'd slept with Sarah.

"I didn't have it planned. JT said I had to go with you." Jack chuckled. "I believe he said, 'Charlie's getting set to make an enormous mistake, Dad. You have to stop him.'"

JT had the grace to look embarrassed. "You weren't supposed to tell him that part, Dad."

"You don't listen to JT. He's a moron," Charlie said, horrified to hear a slight whine in his voice. "You always say that."

"He gave me a grandson, so I figure I owe him one."

JT smirked and flexed. Charlie wanted to kill him, but that would distract him from his main goal, which was to leave his dad home.

"This is stupid. JT, you told me to go to Vegas last week. Remember? I never take vacations? So now I am, and I don't need a babysitter."

"Your brother and I are concerned about your decision making."

"My what?"

"Your career path," JT added.

"I'm not going to Vegas for my career."

"Why are you going again?" his brother asked. "Does it have anything to do with—"

"Don't—" Charlie stopped, frustrated. "Just don't." The three of them were silent. If he kept protesting, someone was going to say Sarah's name, which would make last night even more real, and he couldn't take that. He wanted it swept away. "Fine," he said. "You can come. But you're driving to the airport. And paying for parking."

His dad smiled and held out his hand toward JT, who slapped a stack of twenties into his palm.

"Have fun," his brother said.

"I hate you," Charlie answered.

"I hope you got a good room," Jack said. "I'm not sleeping on a cot."

Charlie decided then and there he was going to figure out a way to ditch his old man before he boarded the plane. Otherwise he might kill him. The unreformed Jack with his bad attitude and quick temper had been hard to take. The smug new Jack was unbearable. Which was more than likely the point. JT wanted to keep him in Statlerville, and he thought by inflicting Jack on him he'd stay home. Well, his dad might be obnoxious, but Charlie was stubborn. He was going to Vegas, and that was final.

After Jack parked at the airport, the two of them rode the shuttle to the terminal in silence. When it got to their stop, Charlie grabbed both bags.

"I'm not an invalid anymore," Jack said, making a move to take his bag back.

"You're slowing me down, old man."

His dad glared at him, but gestured with his hand toward the shuttle doors. "After you, son."

Damn it. He'd been so sure he could piss his dad off enough that he would give up on this stupid idea. With his dad watching his every move, how was he supposed to relax enough to forget last night so he could get back to work on Monday in the right frame of mind? An image of Sarah walking toward him in those wicked, oh-so-wrong-but-oh-so-right heels made his mouth water.

He sighed and got off the shuttle. So his dad was coming. Wasn't like he was going to be able to have any fun, anyway, not with Sarah on his mind.

The line for check-in was long, but Charlie had printed his boarding pass at home so he wouldn't have to wait. Jack had not.

They stood in line behind a group of college boys, all wearing sweatpants and flip-flops, very few of whom appeared to have showered before heading to the airport for a weekend they all agreed was going to be "off the hook."

Charlie kicked his bag along and then shoved Jack's with it.

"Those Finley kids are funny," Jack said. "Simon told me all about your water balloon fight and Lily made me quiz her on the state capitals."

Charlie looked straight ahead. No matter how many times Jack mentioned Sarah or her kids, he was not going to break.

The college boy in front of him, the one wearing the Mets hat, made a remark about how hard he was planning to rock the craps table as soon as he landed. Charlie clenched his fists. The kid should know better than to wear a Mets hat in Philly.

"What's the capital of South Dakota?" Jack asked.

"Pierre," Charlie said. "Is this line even moving?"

Mets Cap made some comment that caused his buddy to shove him. He stepped on Charlie's carry-on. "Oops. Sorry, dude," he said as he straightened.

"How about the capital of Washington? Bet you can't get that one."

"Seattle," Mets Cap guessed.

"Olympia," Charlie said.

"Dude. How do you even know that?" Mets Cap shuffled forward, hitching up his sweatpants. "You must be from there."

Charlie let a gap open between his bags and the college boys. Jack whispered, "Lily knows this song she could teach that kid."

Charlie looked at his watch and sighed. They had enough time to make the plane. They'd be cutting it close, but he thought they could make it.

"Sarah looked fantastic last night," Jack said. "Too bad it was just the two of you."

He couldn't take it. He was supposed to be forgetting about Sarah, but his dad was making that impossible. Leaving town wasn't going to work. He picked up the bags. "You can stop it now." He unhooked the yellow rope from the pole next to him and held it back for his dad to go through.

"Stop what?" Jack asked, stepping slowly through the poles.

Charlie put the rope back and started for the exit doors. "Stop trying to convince me that I would have had a terrible time in Vegas with you and I might as well stay home."

He gave his dad points for trying not to smirk, but in the end, he didn't manage to keep a straight face. "Sorry I'm a bad date."

"I don't get why you couldn't just let me go."

"JT didn't want you to have time to think. Said it's time you started living in the moment."

"I don't need to..." Charlie dropped the bags in frustration. "You know what, Dad? I'm not living in the moment because I have a plan. I made a plan for my life and I've done everything to get myself to exactly where I want to be. Why should I throw all of that away on 'the moment'?"

A woman ushering her family into the terminal pulled her kids closer and made a wide detour around them. *Fantastic.* Now he was scaring whole families.

Jack bent to lift the bags as the shuttle pulled up. Charlie tried to take his back, but his dad waved him off. "I got it."

They managed a disjointed and uninteresting conversation about the Phillies on the ride home. Jack pulled up next to Charlie's car where he'd left it in the hospital garage.

"Your brother doesn't want you to give up your plan, Charlie. And God knows I don't want that. Ever since you were a kid you knew what you wanted and you went for it." Jack paused. "And then you got it. That's not how it works for most of us."

He fiddled with the cup holder. He and his dad didn't talk to each other like this. "Thanks," he managed to say.

"It's the possibility that you might have left some things out of your plan that's got us worried."

He knew better. Don't engage. Walk away. Take the compliment—they were rare on the ground with Jack— and get out. That was the best way to deal with his dad.

"What things?"

"Life."

"What the hell does that mean? I have a plan. It's all about my life."

"No. It's all about your career. All the other parts, the parts that matter, haven't been factored in yet."

Charlie's temper boiled up. He felt himself nodding his head, bobbing it as if he were agreeing with his dad when really he was trying as hard as he could to push his temper back down. "Okay," he said, his neck muscles so tight he could barely breathe. "Thanks again."

"Don't brood," Jack said.

"Don't talk about me with JT anymore."

His dad was smiling again as he drove away. As soon as the car turned the corner, Charlie threw his bag against the front bumper of his car. "I know what I'm doing!" he yelled.

Nobody answered him and Charlie wasn't sure even he believed himself.

SARAH HAD SPENT MOST OF the previous day at Hailey's place, helping Olivia deal with deliveries of flowers and frozen meals and packages wrapped in pastel paper. Earlier she'd managed to extract from JT that Charlie had gone out of town with his father on some family business. They didn't expect him back before late Sunday night. She hoped JT didn't notice that she was asking about Charlie. The guy probably had a bunch of other stuff on his mind besides his brother's sex life, anyway.

She wasn't ready to call him, even just to leave a message. Instead she helped and organized and cleaned until the moment JT pulled up out front with Hailey and Tyrel.

Olivia had helped Lily and Simon make a welcome-home banner that was hanging over the front porch. When Hailey saw it, she cried, and Lily immediately looked over her shoulder. Sarah was pretty sure her daughter was running a quick spell-check.

They all trooped inside, JT in front, carrying the diaper bag over his shoulder while trying to manage two vases of flowers and Sarah's suitcase.

"We have sandwiches and other lunch stuff if you're hungry," she told Hailey.

"I'm starving. But give me a minute. There are some half cousins here who are dying to meet the baby."

She sat in the middle of the couch with Tyrel, and Simon and Lily crowded around them. Hailey un-wrapped the outer blanket and then helped Lily sit back on the couch with the baby in her arms. When Tyrel snuggled closer, Lily shook her head and giggled. She made a kissy face and giggled again. She was the silliest and happiest Sarah had seen her in a long time.

Not wanting to miss anything, Sarah backed toward the bookcase near the door where she thought she'd seen a camera. She bumped into JT, who put his arm across her shoulders, pulling her into a hug. "You have nice kids, Sarah," he said quietly.

She nodded, watching as Hailey transferred Tyrel to Simon's outstretched arms. He didn't get the hang of where to put his hands at first to support Tyrel's neck, but Hailey helped him get it right. He tilted his head from side to side and finally said he had imagined a baby would be bigger.

She leaned her head back against JT's arm. "They're going to spoil your kid rotten."

"Everybody deserves a little something extra sometimes."

Hailey carefully took Tyrel back, handing him off to Olivia, who'd been hovering over the group on the couch, waiting for her turn. She carried her brother closer to the tall, mullioned window near the fireplace, holding him a little away from her body so she could peer at his face. "Who does he look like, Mom? Did I look like this?"

"Not much. You were not a pretty baby."

"Mom!" Olivia said. "How can you say that about your firstborn?"

"It's the truth. You had this shock of black hair that stood straight up off your head."

Simon giggled.

"And your skin was really red."

"Good thing I got better-looking," Olivia said as she bent over to nuzzle her brother. "I think he looks like Uncle Charlie. His eyes are blue, but they're really dark."

Charlie did have exceptional eyes, Sarah thought. Tyrel was a lucky kid if he'd inherited them.

"Most babies have dark eyes. We'll have to wait a few weeks to see if they change," Hailey said.

"Is that true?" JT asked. "How much other stuff don't I know?"

Sarah patted his arm. "You've got all the important stuff."

JT sighed. "Nobody told me how complicated babies would be. He can't even regulate his own body temperature. Very bad design."

Hailey rolled her eyes. "If we're redesigning anything, I vote we start with pregnancy."

"He is perfect," Olivia said. "Even if he doesn't look like me. Hey, where is Uncle Charlie, anyway?"

"He went out of town with your grandpa," JT said, but he was interrupted by the doorbell and then a shout from the porch.

"Anyone home? I've got a present for my grandson!"

Jack McNulty came in with his arms piled full of wrapped gifts. Sarah checked behind him, expecting to see Charlie, but Jack was alone.

So why… But then she realized how stupid she was being. Charlie wasn't with his dad. He never had been with his dad. He probably wasn't even out of town. It was all a lie JT and Hailey had made up to get her to forget about him. She was mortified. Had he asked them to lie?

She stepped away from JT, but he must have seen how uncomfortable she was.

"Dad, I thought you left town with Charlie," he said.

"Decided not to go."

"So then where is he?" Olivia asked.

Jack dropped the packages on the wing chair near the fireplace and then lifted Tyrel out of Olivia's arms.

"I dropped him off yesterday. Haven't seen him since."

She couldn't stay here. They were all so happy and so together and okay. She was pretty sure now they hadn't been lying to her, otherwise Jack would have had a better story, but she was also sure Charlie had been in town all weekend and he hadn't called for no good reason. That hurt. He could have at least said thank-you for the party.

She made it through another five minutes, but then gathered the kids and went home.

That night Sarah found *The Sound of Music* on TV and she finally did have the breakdown Hailey had been bugging her about. Not over Erik, or Lauren and Erik, or her own lost dreams for her family. She wasn't even crying over Simon or her worries for him, which never seemed far from her mind these days.

Instead, she sat alone in her dark living room and cried about the Captain and Maria in the movie, how close they came to missing each other. How it could have all gone wrong if they'd made different choices. By the time the Von Trapps were hiking up the Alps, carrying the children piggyback, Sarah felt wept out and determined not to let her chance pass her by. She'd felt a connection with Charlie and she was going to find out what that meant. She couldn't let him slip away without at least giving it a try. He might be too...too whatever to call her, but she wouldn't take the easy way out this time.

And yet, when Monday morning came around, she put off calling him. She decided to mop the kitchen floor. The white tile Erik had insisted on showed every stray poppy seed and drop of jelly with unflinching starkness.

The floor needed to be mopped.

She wasn't, she thought as she filled the bucket, old-fashioned about women's roles or anything. She could have called him, especially because he was hiding out at home. But she was the one who was recently divorced. It had been years since she'd called a guy.

She squirted some tile cleaner on the area in front of the fridge and then shoved her damp mop through it.

Shouldn't Charlie be aware of that, and therefore, shouldn't he be the one to pick up the phone? Wasn't he the one who'd been dating all these years? She'd seen him at Baxter Smiley functions and charity events with at least four different beautiful women since he'd started with the firm after grad school. There might be count-less others. Throngs of women. He must have called at least some of those women, right?

A stubborn stain near the island refused to budge for the mop so she got down and scrubbed at it with a rag. Then she wiped the baseboards of the island and rubbed a few fingerprints off the lower cupboards. The monstrous island stood much too high for her to use as a prep station, and topped with black granite, it sucked the light out of the room. Ugly or not, the island didn't have to be dirty.

Charlie should be the one to call because he would know what to say in that sexy, 900-number voice.

She wrung the mop out, pushing the lever down and holding it tight as she watched the last few drops of water fall into the bucket.

She could figure out what to say if she had to. She wasn't a total buffoon. Heck, if she searched Google for "call a man after strip poker" she'd probably find six or seven how-to guides. The Internet was an astonishingly specific place.

But wouldn't it be easier if he picked up the phone first? Easier because she wouldn't have to figure out what to say. She wouldn't have to be the one who made the first move.

Because she would know what he wanted without having to let him know what she wanted first.

She pushed the mop across the last dirty spots in front of the sink and then lifted the bucket, letting the dirty water splash down into the deep sink. She watched it swirl around the drain and then used the hose to rinse everything down.

Okay. She was a chicken. And acting like a thirteen-year-old girl with her first crush. But Charlie wasn't a chicken. So why didn't he just call, already? Why had he been home all weekend in his apartment and never picked up the phone? Had he decided they couldn't work things out? She knew he had that partnership issue, and the trouble with the kids and school, and she worried that he didn't trust her. She didn't like the idea that the changes she'd made, her new dedication to living life on her terms, bothered Charlie the most. She liked him. She wanted to be with him. But not if she had to go back to being who she'd been.

She grabbed the throw rug and headed for the basement stairs. She would figure this out. She was absolutely going to pick up the phone and call him. Right after she put in a load of darks.

"MOM, LILY PROMISED SHE'D play with me but now she won't," Simon said. He slumped onto a stool at the kitchen island where she'd been reading an old *People* magazine and trying not to think about calling Charlie.

Simon was wearing the reindeer tie again and a pair of Erik's old sunglasses with the lenses popped out. Lily, who'd followed him into the room, had on striped stockings and a purple tutu and an armful of plastic bangle bracelets Sarah had won as a gag gift at a wedding shower a few years ago.

"Honey, why won't you play with your brother?"

"Because there's nothing good to do. Everything is boring."

The long days alone were getting to the kids. Especially Lily. When a person was used to conquering the world, or at least the fourth grade, on a daily basis, it was hard to retire gracefully.

"What would make it not boring?"

Lily did a twirl and then another one. "He wants to play that he's going to an office, but I want to be a princess and they don't go to offices. And besides, we don't have any princess stuff."

They didn't have any princess stuff because Lily had sworn she was over dressing up. She'd packed up most of her outfits and given them to Danielle Simmons's younger daughter. But now, with only Simon around for company, she was getting desperate, apparently.

"I have a tiara. You want that?" She had no idea what made her remember it just then, but the eager look on Lily's face made her glad she had.

"Let's go," Sarah said. "It's in my trunk in the attic."

The three of them trooped up the stairs to the third floor where the big attic ceiling fan spun quietly. The air was still warmer than downstairs, though, and Sarah felt prickles of sweat on the back of her neck.

"But why did you get a tiara if you didn't win?" Lily asked. "Don't they only give them out to the winners?"

"Usually," Sarah agreed.

Sarah knelt down next to the steamer trunk she'd been using to store her memories ever since she'd been just a little bit older than Lily. She'd found it in her grandmother's attic one day and had been allowed to bring it home.

She kept the key on a nail next to the trunk. It was still tied on a rainbow-striped shoelace she'd rescued from a pair of sneakers she'd outgrown. Looping the lace on one finger, she dangled the key in front of Simon. "You want to open it?"

He took it eagerly.

"Mom? How did you get a tiara? Was it for first runner-up?" Lily seemed not to have even noticed that her little brother was getting to work the key in the lock, focused as she was on the one aspect of the pageant experience that mattered to her—winning.

"I have two," Sarah said. "One is a runner-up tiara.

In that pageant I won the talent portion and they handed out tiaras for each section winner. The other one is for first place."

Lily put a hand on her hip, flattening the lilac tulle tutu against her striped tights. "You won a pageant? When Grandma used to tell me stories she said you always came in second."

Simon had the trunk opened so Sarah started rooting around for the tiara boxes. "I didn't always come in second."

At Lily's skeptical look, Sarah said, "Sometimes I came in third and a whole bunch of times I didn't place at all."

"Mom," Lily said.

"Sorry."

And she actually was sorry, in a way. Lily's focus on being the best had always made her uneasy. Her daughter was a very successful person, but she cared so much. Sarah worried about what would happen to her when she ran into her first disappointment. So she often found herself teasing Lily about winning, maybe in an effort to show her it was okay to be second-best. Except, she was uneasy with that lesson, too. How many mothers would try to give their children the gift of being satisfied with mediocre?

Simon pulled out a red cape she'd used in a tap routine. "Can I have this?"

"Sure," Sarah said, glad for the distraction. "Oh, here."

The velvet boxes were eighteen years old. She'd stopped entering pageants when she was sixteen and her mother had finally understood that there wasn't going to be a sudden growth spurt to transform her into someone who was willowy, curvaceous and tall. In other words, someone who had a valid shot at coming in first. She'd been ecstatic initially about all her newfound free time. But after a while she realized that without the pageants she didn't have much in common with her mom. Her last two years at home had been lonely, and she'd eagerly escaped the house for school activities and later to Villanova.

"Here's the dance one."

She opened the midnight-blue box. Simon was leaning on her shoulder and even Lily had crouched down next to her.

"Mom, that's beautiful," Lily said quietly.

Sarah lifted it out, the crystals glittering in the silver-plated setting. Of course Lily, who hadn't yet grown out of her princess-worshipping fashion phase despite what she might say, thought it was beautiful. It was undeniably sparkly. She put it on her daughter's head and sat back on her heels.

"It suits you, Lily," she said.

Simon put one finger out to set the tiny crystal hanging from the raised center section swinging. "Can she really wear it to play?"

Sarah nodded. "Yep. That's exactly what she should do with it."

"Open the other one," Lily said, holding her head carefully still. Sarah flicked the small brass clasp with her fingernail and tilted back the lid of the burgundy velvet box.

The tiara inside was slightly bigger than the one she'd given Lily, but was still more "afternoon tea with the duchess" than "coronation of the queen" size.

"You want to wear this one, Simon?" she asked.

He made a sour face. "I'm not a girl." He patted his tie and said in a deep voice, "There are no tiaras in the office."

"Who says?" Sarah lifted it out and settled it on his head, but he made a face so she put it on herself.

Hands on her hips, she tossed her head in a fair imitation of her old pageant pose. She'd been messing around, but when she looked at her kids, they were staring at her, their eyes wide.

"Mom, you look beautiful," Lily said. She climbed to her feet, arms out to balance herself, and walked quickly but carefully, one foot exactly in front of the other, like Eliza Doolittle in her deportment class, to the mirror on the back of the attic door. "Tiaras are magic."

Sarah crossed the floor to stand behind her daughter. Simon came up next to her and put his arm around her waist. The three of them looked at themselves in the mirror. Sarah hadn't had a tiara on her head in years. She was floored to find that she got a kick out of the tiara now when she'd never enjoyed it before. She'd always been ashamed of her prizes; she'd gotten one by default in a competition in which she'd placed fourth but the first three competitors were disqualified for cheating. The actual winner had used a voice enhancer during the talent competition. The first runner-up and her mother had stolen the specially dyed-to-match turquoise heels the second runner-up had intended to wear with her final dress. She had retaliated by slashing the first runner-up's hair extensions.

After she won, her mom had wanted to have her portrait done in the sash and tiara. Sarah had refused because she'd known that while she was certainly Little Miss Wouldn't Stoop to Cheating, she was not rightfully Miss Teen Southeastern Pennsylvania.

In the eyes of her kids, though, she was beautiful. Ms. Best in Attic. They expected her to be a winner, to be the one who knew what was going on, to protect them.

"Let's have a pageant," she said.

"I'm not a *girl*." Simon sounded irritated at how often he'd needed to remind them of that.

"This can be a boys and girls pageant. Even better, let's make it a talent show." Lily looked interested and so Sarah pushed on. This would fill the afternoon, at least. "Everybody find a spot in the attic to be private. We'll take three minutes to think of a talent and then we'll meet back here for the show."

Neither of the kids would go first, so Sarah took her tiara off and handed it to Lily. The kids seated themselves on the lid of the trunk. She cleared her throat. "My talent is dance," she announced as she started humming, and then she launched into a boisterous macarena. After she'd gone through the dance four times, she stopped and the kids applauded.

"Who's next?"

Lily jumped up. "My talent is the state capitals song," she said, and then raced through the capitals sung to a tune with the unmistakable stamp of elementary school music class all over it. She went from Baton Rouge to Carson City, taking about three breaths along the way and pausing only long enough for an enthusiastic spin move on Sa-a-acramento, California. When she finished, Sarah and Simon both clapped. Lily bowed.

Simon got up slowly. He squeezed the bottom of the reindeer tie and stared at it while "Up on the House-top" played. Sarah hoped that wasn't his talent because she very much feared his sister would say something scathing.

"That's not my talent," he said after the song ended. "That was my intro song."

"All right, then, what is your talent?" Lily asked.

"Jokes."

Sarah's heart sank. She had heard Simon's jokes before and they weren't a hit with Lily. Why had she proposed this stupid game? She shot a look at Lily to warn her to be nice, but her daughter was watching Simon with what seemed like polite attention.

"What did the dentist say when his wife made a cake?"

Lily shrugged and Sarah said, "We give up."

"He said, 'Can I do the filling?'"

Not bad. He got a smile out of his sister, at least. Sarah started to stand up, but he said, "One more." He shuffled his feet. "What did the traffic light say to the car?"

"We don't know."

Simon crossed his legs and put his hand over his chest and squeaked, "Don't look, I'm changing."

Lily fell off the trunk laughing. Sarah laughed, too, not because the joke was funny, although Simon had looked hilarious when he delivered the punch line, but because the kids were both laughing so hard they couldn't speak. Silly jokes really were a kid thing. Something to share with your sibling.

She put her tiara back on and helped Lily to her feet. She led them back to stand in front of the mirror, where she squeezed Lily's shoulder and pressed a kiss on top of Simon's head.

"We look good," she said. And they did. Lily in her striped tights, purple tutu and tiara; Simon with the long reindeer tie and the red cape; and she in a pair of old jeans, leather flip-flops and her tiara. They looked perfect. They were perfect.

She wished she had a camera, because she wanted to take a self-timer picture so she could capture this moment. She'd remember it because it was exactly the moment that she knew what she needed to do. She'd been uncomfortable about the plans for the kids, the good-behavior pledge and the probation in particular. So they weren't going back. Erik would be furious, and she'd probably lose some friends. More friends. More people who'd only pretended to be friends. But she wanted her kids to grow up free. She didn't want them constantly trying to measure up. So that was the gift she'd give them. From now on, Sarah and her kids were doing exactly what they wanted.

"Who won?" Lily asked.

"It was a tie," Sarah told her. "Three for first place."

"I knew you were going to say that," Lily said. "But I think it kind of was, for real, not just because moms can't have favorites."

Sarah nodded. The suspension hadn't been all bad, she realized. Lily and Simon had spent so much time together that his sister had learned to appreciate him more. He'd always admired Lily, but now it seemed as if she understood her brother, and not just in a tolerant way, but in a genuinely interested one. Maybe if he could start over somewhere new he'd find other kids who'd be willing to give him a chance.

As they headed downstairs, she decided she liked the way the tiara felt. Maybe Lily was right and it really was magic. Or maybe she'd finally grown into it. Whatever, she didn't feel like taking it off just yet.

CHAPTER TEN

ERIK FINLEY'S OFFICE didn't suit him. The office was classy, understated and inviting. Erik was none of those things. Charlie had been sitting across the desk from him for almost forty-five minutes, plenty of time to catalog the man's defects. And they were many.

Charlie was as fond of lists as most portfolio managers. He liked to collect facts, background, inside tips and comparisons of historical data. Part of why he was good at what he did was that he could look past the numbers and see the story. It was a rare investor who was disciplined enough to buy or sell based on numbers. Most of them were looking for a story. Charlie had learned how to put the story and the numbers together into a package that his clients found hard to turn down.

In the past forty-five minutes, the list he'd compiled about Erik was long and detailed. The executive summary would read, "Arrogant for no good reason. Tendency to be a dick. Prone to inappropriate sharing about sexual exploits with boss, now second wife."

Charlie drummed his fingers on the arm of the chair. He'd known all those things about Erik before. But this morning they were grating on him like an exposed nail on the seat of his chair. It must be because Erik had been gone for so long.

Unless it was because of Erik's ex-wife. And her black bra...

"So the last thing is this business with the school. Did you talk to Ryan about it?"

Charlie added "bad father" to his list. "We talked," he said, hoping to cut this as short as possible. "I was there when he met with the principal. He's satisfied with the plan."

"Do you need to touch base with him again? Reassure him that the kids are ready to go back? That they've learned their lesson?"

"I don't think I should be involved, Erik. It's your family's private business."

"You're already involved. You've got Ryan on the hook and you're on the board. How much more involved can you get?"

I could sleep with Sarah.

"If we don't have any more business, I'm going to head back to my office."

Erik dropped his pen on the desk blotter. "You don't get to decide when the meeting is over. I'm the partner here. You might want to remember that."

"I'm not comfortable talking about your family."

"Until the Ryan deal is squared away, my family is part of your life."

Charlie's fists were clenched on his thighs. He carefully unclenched them, relaxing his jaw and taking a deep breath. Erik was necessary; he wasn't allowed to antagonize the man.

"I'm sure things are going to be fine."

"And I'm equally sure Sarah and Simon have screwed our chances with Ryan. I'm telling you, Charlie, those two are a mystery to me. How the same genes could produce Lily and Simon, I can't understand. I'm furious with Sarah."

Charlie's anger, which he'd just carefully banked, flared. When he'd played football, he'd had a few rare moments of total clarity—the field and the crowd all evaporated until it was just him, the ball and one receiver. A similar thing happened to him now. He lost all the details of the office; his focus narrowed to his fist and Erik's face.

He was halfway out of his chair, his fist cocked back and every muscle bunched to launch himself over the desk, before he realized what he was doing. Erik was frozen in his chair, his face drained of color. Charlie forced his hand back to his side. He put it in his pocket for good measure and used his left hand to straighten his tie.

He couldn't believe he'd almost punched Erik. Not that the guy didn't deserve it, but he wasn't just a jerk, he was Erik Finley, partner at Baxter Smiley, and Lauren Smiley's husband. Charlie lowered himself back into the chair, focusing on the resistance in each muscle, pushing everything Erik had said about Sarah to the fringe.

"Um," Erik said, "I didn't mean to upset you. It's possible the account will be fine. I…uh…I guess that's it."

Charlie practically dove for the door. Before he could leave, though, Erik called his name. When he turned, Erik had his hands folded on his desk, his composure back in place.

"Lauren and I discussed the firm while we were away. We're having a meeting later this week with all the partners. I'm sure you know what that means. Keep up the good work."

Erik winked. The wink and the coy closing statement sent Charlie's temper through the roof. Erik thought he'd been mad about the deal. He thought they were on the same godforsaken wavelength. The man had no idea how close he'd been to receiving a full-bore McNulty butt-kicking. Not that he'd personally beaten anyone up since high school. But he didn't have to do it habitually to know who'd win if he did decide to throw down with Erik.

He returned to his office and closed his door gently. As soon as the solid wood was between him and the rest of the firm, Charlie gave his metal garbage can a savage kick. His breathing was uneven as he contemplated the mess he'd made.

He only wished it had been Erik's head and not a garbage can. How dare that creep say one word about Sarah? And bringing a six-year-old boy into things was just wrong. Dirty, dirty pool. That the kid was Erik's own son made his stomach turn.

He needed to get out of there for a while, but he couldn't go home to his empty apartment. He needed to do something to work out his anger. He had to release some of his emotions before he dug himself a deeper hole at work.

The trouble was, his life was built on being in control at all times, in all situations. He didn't have an escape hatch. There was nowhere he felt comfortable being anything less than rational.

Except. His nerves tingled at the thought of her. The couple of times they'd been together, he'd been able to let loose—dancing, the water fight, Vegas night. What would it feel like if he went to her on purpose, looking for a release? Would she be able to keep up with him? Would she want to?

He picked up his phone and dialed her number. But then he hung up. He was not getting involved with Sarah. The partners were meeting sometime next week. He just needed to hold on until then, and after the meeting, after his partnership was in the bag, then he could take some time and work off this whatever the hell it was that was eating at him. For now, though, he thought he'd head home. Olivia had been bugging him to take her driving. Maybe a brush with death at the hands of a novice teenage driver would calm his nerves.

When he walked out, it was early and he didn't even take any files with him. He'd been leaving early quite a bit recently, and even though he told himself he was going to work at home, most nights he didn't. He spent his evenings in front of the TV, watching the Phillies piss away the beginning of their season.

He'd been over to JT's a couple of times. Hailey had gone back to normal and he wasn't so worried he was going to drop Tyrel anymore and actually enjoyed holding him, but he couldn't make himself stay. Something about being there in the middle of the family they'd made with each other left him restless. Olivia had noticed. The last time he went she asked him if he was feeling okay and he'd had to fake a smile. Being with JT's family wasn't enough. Nothing was enough.

He missed Sarah. He missed her kids. He wondered what they were up to, and he found himself making excuses to drive past her house. But he hadn't been hit with any water balloons. Sometimes he wondered if they were out of town, but he had no way of knowing.

If only he could move on.

He called JT's, but Hailey told him Olivia was out with friends. He didn't feel like going home and was going to go nuts if he didn't find something to do, so he drove around, hoping he might see Olivia hanging out somewhere.

He'd just circled the elementary school when he passed a kid trudging along the sidewalk in a green-and-white baseball uniform, a huge equipment bag slung over her hunched back. He took another look in the rearview mirror and something about the precision-tied green-and-white bow tied around the blond ponytail sticking out the back of the cap was familiar to him.

At the next corner, he made a U-turn and went back. He pulled up alongside Lily and rolled the window down. She looked first startled by the car and then wary, edging away from the street as she picked up her pace. He rolled the car forward and called, "Lily, it's Charlie McNulty."

She recognized him and stopped walking, but she still didn't approach the car.

"Where are you going?" he asked.

"I have a game on the high school fields." She shifted the bag. He could see the sharp line the straps were cutting into her hand.

"What's in the bag? The rest of the team?"

"I'm the catcher."

So pads, then, he guessed. Probably a bat. But from the size of the bag he wondered if she wasn't also carrying her own bases. Or the scoreboard.

"How come you're walking? Wouldn't your mom give you a ride?"

She stared over the top of the car. "I like to walk."

Right.

He studied her for a second and then leaned over to push the passenger-side door open. "Hop in, I can drop you."

She stepped back so fast she tripped and almost went down. She swung around sideways so the bag was between her and the car. "No, no thanks."

It was hot. She was sweaty. The bag was heavy and the fields were still at least a half mile away.

"Why not?"

"I can't get in your car. You know…stranger danger."

Stranger danger? He started to smile, but then realized this wasn't a joke to her. So. He remembered now that JT had told him a code word he was supposed to use if he ever had to pick Olivia up when she wasn't expecting it. He'd bet anything that Sarah had a code word, too, for her kids, but of course you didn't tell the code word to the guy you weren't even actually dating. Code word or not, he couldn't let Lily carry the damn bag all the way to the fields.

"How about I take the bag? You keep walking and I'll meet you there."

She let the bag slide down from her shoulder to the sidewalk. Shaking her hand out, she studied him, her face serious. Was she weighing the possibilities that he might steal her gear? She reached a decision.

"Okay." Hefting the bag again, she brought it to the car and slid it into the passenger seat. It was an awkward fit and the bag ended up wedged into the seat almost as if it were a person sitting next to him.

He patted the bag as she stepped back. "All set, then. The high school?"

She nodded and closed the door. He leaned around the bag to call through the still-open window. "You're a smart kid, Lily."

She shrugged. Apparently she already knew that. An alert started pinging because his passenger wasn't wearing a seat belt. He reached around the bag and buckled it in just to shut the noise up.

Without the bag, she moved a lot quicker and he was able to drive slowly enough to keep her in his rearview mirror the whole way. She caught up to him in the parking lot and took the bag. He checked the fields but didn't see any other green-and-white uniforms. He didn't see anyone else except one older guy in a baseball cap standing near the pitcher's mound.

"Are you sure your game is today?" he asked.

She looked over her shoulder. "That's Coach Pete. I like to get here early so he can help me warm up." A car pulled in and another girl got out. "That's our starting pitcher. She needs to work on her inside stuff." She grabbed the bag, ducking and lifting to get it up on her shoulder again. "Thanks, Mr. McNulty. I appreciate it."

He sat for a few seconds in the parking lot, watching her head for the dugout, where she settled on the bench to start dressing. The coach said something to her and she responded, but he couldn't hear what it was. Probably an apology for being late, even though she'd been the first one there. Of course she liked to get there early—it was exactly the way he'd been when he was a kid. If you got there early, you got extra time with the coach, extra time to warm up and had plenty of time to scope out the other team when they showed up.

What bugged him was that she'd been walking alone. What the hell was Sarah thinking? This was exactly the kind of crap his parents had pulled when he and JT were kids. His mom and dad's lives had been all about them; whatever whim or drama was driving the moment always took precedence over the stuff that mattered to him and his brother. This practice mattered to Lily, but she'd had to schlep her own gear when it was much too hot and she was much too little.

He'd been mad at Erik earlier in the office and determined to get his life back. Now all of his anger shifted to Sarah. Why couldn't she get her act together?

He pulled out his phone and called her number, but she didn't pick up. He checked the field one more time. Lily was in her crouch behind the plate. The girl on the mound pitched one in low and fast and she grabbed it, the ball making a sweet thud into the leather.

Charlie backed out of the lot, intending to head home, but he found himself on Sarah's street. He wasn't going to stop, but when he saw her SUV in the driveway, he pulled in behind it.

She thought she was living this new life where she

did what she wanted, but there were things you couldn't do when kids were involved.

He banged on the door.

SHE WAS IN THE KITCHEN cleaning the floor again and hating every square inch of the white tile more with each stroke of her rag. The kids had used colored chalk to turn the patio into a mosaic earlier in the week and it was beautiful, but the chalk kept getting tracked into the house.

When she heard the banging on the front door, she guessed it was Erik, coming to tell her he was taking Lily. Late again, she thought sourly.

"Simon, go see if that's Dad at the door, would you?" she called.

When she heard Simon say, "Hello, Mr. McNulty. You want to throw more water balloons?" she put down the rag she'd been using to clean the floor and dried her hands. Why did he have to show up unannounced? She'd been hoping he would call and instead here he was and she looked like, well, she looked like a person who'd just spent twenty minutes on her knees scrubbing the kitchen floor.

"Is your mom here?" So of course she had to go see him.

She walked up behind Simon, trying to be cool. "Charlie?" The cool evaporated as soon as she got close to him. He was wearing dark suit pants and a blue-and-white-striped shirt with the sleeves rolled up to his elbows. His dark blond hair caught the sun at the temples. She should have been pissed that he was so sophisticated when she was so disheveled, but instead she was turned on as she remembered watching him strip out of a very similar striped shirt the other night. "I… Hello… What are you doing here?"

"Can I talk to you for a second?" He stepped back to give her space to open the screen. "Alone?"

Simon sighed. "I'm going." He started down the hall but paused to say, "I hate grown-up talks."

Sarah smoothed her hands across the seat of her jeans and pushed her headband back in place before coming out to join him on the porch. "I'm sorry I didn't call you," she said. "I thought…when you didn't call that you didn't want—"

"Do you know where Lily is?" he interrupted.

She flinched at his tone. "At her baseball game."

"Yeah, she's there now, no thanks to you."

She had no idea why he was mad, but she wasn't feeling happy to see him anymore. "What are you talking about, Charlie?" She opened the screen door and pulled the inside door shut so Simon wouldn't hear whatever he had to say.

"I'm talking about Lily and you making her walk to the game even though it must be two miles from here and she has that ridiculous gear bag full of God knows what. What could you possibly have been doing that was so important you couldn't give her a ride?"

Oh, no. She wasn't going to take that from Charlie. Not after he didn't call or even acknowledge that the last time they'd seen each other, she'd been naked and he'd been creeping out of her guest house.

"First of all, Erik gave her a ride. Baseball is his thing. Second, you don't get to talk to me about my kids this way. Third, you don't get to talk to me at all." She spun on her heel to go into the house, but he put a hand on her elbow, stopping her.

"Erik was supposed to take her?"

"Erik *did* take her. He picked her up a few minutes ago." Granted, she hadn't actually seen him pull up, but Lily had been waiting outside and she…and she…she must have… Lily would never go with someone else or just take off without telling her mother. She knew better.

"I saw her walking and offered her a ride."

A chill swept over her. She needed to see Lily now. "She was walking by herself? To the high school?"

Charlie shrugged. "I thought…"

"She got in your car?" Sarah felt terrified. "Why would she do that? She knows better. Did she even ask you for the code word?" She turned around and pulled the screen door open and then pushed the inside door. "Simon!" she yelled. "Get your shoes."

Charlie shifted uncomfortably. "She's okay, Sarah. Her coach was at the field and she didn't get in my car." He shook his head. "I'm still in the potentially dangerous stranger category. I took her bag, that was it."

"Right." She cupped her hands and yelled louder, "Simon. Move it!" Pulling her phone out of her jeans, she called Erik, muttering, "I'm going to kill him. I can't believe he'd leave her hanging." She listened to the phone ring. "Pick up, jackass." She got his voice mail and snapped the phone shut with a curse.

Simon skidded down the hall and bumped into her hip. "Mom, you said a bad word. Is Mr. McNulty in trouble?"

"No. We're going to your sister's game."

She grabbed her purse off the hall table and then came back out onto the porch. Charlie was still standing there, but when she and Simon came flying out, he gave them space. She was halfway across the yard when she said, "Thanks for looking out for her, Charlie. Can you move your car?" She was in her car with the door closed without even looking to see if he'd answered.

YES, MA'AM. MOVE THE CAR. Charlie jogged across the lawn and backed out. He pulled his Mercedes forward on the street so she'd have room to turn behind him. He watched in his mirror as she backed down the driveway and headed for the high school, her speed not quite high enough to get a ticket, but not exactly sedate.

Now he was going home.

Because…

Because nothing. There was nothing waiting for him there. He made his second U-turn of the day and followed the now-familiar route back to the high school. It had been a long time since he'd watched a live baseball game and it turned out he was in exactly the right mood for Little League.

WHEN SARAH GOT TO THE FIELD, she was so keyed up she was shaking. Erik was still not answering his phone. Where was he? How dare he stand Lily up? She pulled into a space near the fence and then got out, calling to Simon to wait for her in the bleachers as she ran to the field where Lily and Coach Pete were working out.

"Lily," she called.

Her daughter jumped at the sound of her voice but

still managed to catch the ball coming at her. Sarah jogged up to the plate just as Lily stood and tipped back her catcher's helmet.

Her daughter's face was sweaty. Strands of blond hair were plastered across her forehead. A streak of dirt ran from her ear down under her chin where she'd probably scratched an itch with her glove on. There wasn't one thing about her that wasn't precious to Sarah. She pulled her daughter into a hug, wrapping her arms around her, chest protector, shin guards, helmet and all.

"Mom." Lily wiggled. "Coach is throwing to me."

Sarah released her. "Why did you walk here?" She sounded hysterical, but she didn't care. She *was* hysterical, and maybe it wasn't a bad thing for Lily to know it. "You're not allowed to walk this far on your own."

"Dad didn't come," Lily muttered. "I didn't want to be late."

"I would have driven you. I was right inside."

"What's up, Mrs. Finley?" Pete Thomas asked. He'd come halfway between the mound and home plate. His kids were older than hers so she didn't know him well. He coached the girls' baseball team at the high school and liked to work with the up-and-coming players in the travel league where he coached every summer.

"Please, call me Sarah," she said distractedly, but then added, "I just need to speak with Lily for a minute." She put an arm around her daughter's shoulders, reluctant to let her go. "I'll have her back in a sec."

They walked toward the backstop and Sarah leaned down close. "How did this happen, Lily?"

"Dad didn't come and I knew if I told you…well…I didn't want you to find out."

"But walking all the way here on your own? With that bag? I could have driven you, no problem. Did you think I wouldn't take you?"

Lily looked down, but her hands were clenched into fists and her voice was low when she answered. "I didn't want you to fight with him. He's supposed to take me and I thought you'd be mad."

Sarah took a breath. She would have been mad. She *was* mad. She was pretty sure she had every right to be mad, but there was more to look at here. "I would have been mad, you're right. But I would have driven you."

"I didn't want you to know because you don't understand. You wish I wouldn't play because you think all I care about is winning. I heard you telling Dad that I need to have a healthier attitude. But I like to play. I like to win, too, but I like to play. If Dad stops bringing me and you're in charge, you'll make me quit. It'll be just like you making me switch schools. But I'm not like you and Simon. This is what I'm like."

Sarah put her hand to her mouth. "Oh, Lil," she said. "Oh, baby. I'm sorry."

Lily shrugged one shoulder. There were tears in her eyes, but she was too proud or too stubborn to wipe them away. Sarah put her thumbs on her daughter's cheeks and gently dried the tears.

"I've been tough on you."

Lily nodded.

"Okay," Sarah said. She moved her hands to Lily's shoulders. "Okay. I'll figure this out with your dad.

You're right. I think this is too serious. You're only nine and should be…daydreaming but…we'll figure it out."

"Figure it out so I can play?"

"Promise."

"Even if you have to drive me to the games?" Lily sounded skeptical. "Because some of them are pretty far away."

"I promise," Sarah repeated. "But you have to promise not to go off on your own. You can't hide things from me. Seriously, Lily. We have to work together."

"Okay." Lily's attention was already shifting back to the plate. "Can I go now?"

Sarah lifted her hands. "Have fun."

Lily shot her a look.

"Do your best?"

"Mom!"

"Fine. Crush them like a grape."

Her daughter's wide, happy grin was all the answer Sarah needed. She'd done this right at last. Now she needed to figure out how to keep their new life where they made smarter choices.

CHARLIE TOOK A SEAT on the bleachers next to Simon. The kid sat forward with his arms on his knees, chin in his hands. Other kids and parents were starting to filter in now, but Simon was focused on his mom and sister standing near the backstop. Charlie didn't interrupt him. The two of them sat and watched until they saw Lily laugh and jog back to the plate. Simon let out a breath and leaned back.

"Looks like they sorted things out," Charlie said.

"Yeah," Simon agreed. "My mom can fix anything."

Charlie studied the kid. He was on the skinny side, his knees were scraped and his hair was sticking out as if he hadn't exactly subdued it that morning. His big black diver's watch was strapped on his left wrist. He was wearing green shorts and a red T-shirt and his socks were covered with multicolored smudges, maybe from paint.

In other words, he looked perfectly normal. Like an ordinary, well-cared-for little kid. Charlie watched him watch his mom and he understood that Sarah was worlds away from his own mom. This wasn't a kid growing up in the midst of damaging drama, even if he was growing up in a house where things weren't always entirely normal.

Charlie wondered what that was like. Sarah seemed to have shrugged off some of the rules about what was expected of her, but she hadn't gone entirely out of bounds.

She came back and sat on the bleacher in front of them. "I didn't expect to see you here," she said to Charlie as she pulled a sticky burr off Simon's sock.

"I wasn't planning to come," he said.

"But…?"

"But I…I guess I wanted to see…um…how things went."

She turned to him and touched his knee. "Thanks again, Charlie. For looking out for her and for telling me."

"Sorry I jumped to conclusions."

She didn't answer right away. But then with a glance at Simon she said, "Don't worry about it."

He could tell she didn't exactly mean that. And he was worried about it. He just didn't know what to do about it.

They sat in uncomfortable silence for about fifteen minutes while families filled in the seats around them. Still no sign of Erik. He saw Sarah check her phone a few times.

A couple of boys around Simon's age were playing catch behind the bleachers. Charlie saw the kid watching them. "Those guys friends of yours?" he asked.

"They go to my school. My school that I'm suspended from."

"You don't have your glove with you?"

"I don't feel like playing," Simon said. But the way his eyes tracked the boys, Charlie didn't think that was the truth. He guessed Simon worried he wouldn't be allowed to play if he went over there.

"But you do have your glove?"

Simon nodded. "Lily says to keep it in the car because then I'm always ready." He realized what he'd said then and tried to backpedal. "If I wanted to play. Which I don't."

"That's a bummer," Charlie said. "I thought you might throw a couple with me."

"You want to play catch?" Simon asked, with so much skepticism that Charlie actually stopped to make sure he was answering honestly.

"Yeah," he said. "I do."

Sarah mouthed "thank you" to him as he went past, and the funny thing was, he was irritated. He wasn't doing the kid a favor. He had other ways to fill his time. He wasn't sure exactly what, but he was a grown man. He was tossing the ball with Simon because he wanted to. End of story.

Simon was about as accurate with a baseball as he'd

been with the water balloons, but once they moved far enough away from the stands that he wasn't in danger of hitting anybody, he seemed to enjoy himself. Charlie gave him a couple of pointers, reminded him to get his arm back, and showed him how to use his glove to point toward the target. By the time the game was getting ready to start, Simon's throws were wobbling a little straighter and the acrobatics required for Charlie to catch his first few weren't necessary as often.

Charlie caught the last one and called to Simon, "Want to get a hot dog?"

Simon's face lit up. "Yes, I do."

So another way Simon was just like every other male of the species, Charlie thought as he dropped a hand on the kid's shoulder to usher him back toward the snack stand.

"Your mom like hot dogs?" he asked as they ordered.

Simon nodded. "She used to only eat the veggie dogs from Whole Foods, but now she eats the regular ones, which Lily says have pig hair in them, but I don't care because at least they don't have veggies in them."

Charlie laughed. Veggie dogs sounded disgusting. Pig hair didn't sound all that appetizing, either, but he figured he'd been eating hot dogs for enough years that if they were going to kill him, it would have already happened. He asked for a large order of fries, anyway, just in case, but it turned out Simon was right and Sarah did like hot dogs, too, possible pig hair and all.

SARAH HAD NO IDEA WHY he stayed. At first everything was fine. He played catch with Simon, which was something Erik hadn't done in weeks, as far as she knew. Then he bought them hot dogs and fries. He and Simon invented names for the players on the opposing team, like Blue Legs and Drops 'Em All. The names weren't exactly nice, but they were funny and it kept Simon engaged in the game.

Charlie kept asking her questions she couldn't answer about Lily's team. Things about their averages and win/loss percentage and how long Pete Thomas had been coaching. He didn't seem to get that she didn't watch that way. She liked to watch her girl play this game she was good at. She liked to soak up the early-evening sun. That was about it.

"What is he thinking?" Charlie muttered. He was leaning forward, focusing intently on the action at the plate. Sarah had no idea what he was seeing. She glanced around. Tom Corey and Dave Simmons were sitting two rows down and both were leaning forward the same way Charlie was. They were two of the parents who drove her nuts, always yelling at their kids or the umpire. Malcolm Donnelly, one of the partners from Baxter Smiley, whose daughter played right field, was also looking tense in his lawn chair near the fence. Danielle Simmons was sitting next to her husband, but she hadn't spoken to Sarah or even made eye contact. She wasn't sure if Danielle was still nursing a grudge about the strawberry shortcakes or if she'd written her off for good.

In fact, none of the other parents had spoken to her. It was as if she and Simon were an island, a leper colony. Well, she and Simon and Charlie, who was still there.

Right behind her. Watching the game and catching French fries in his mouth, much to her son's delight.

She didn't want to read too much into him being there, but the truth couldn't be disputed. He was there and she was there and they were sharing dinner. An optimistic sort of person might have called it a date. After days of not hearing from him, she wouldn't call herself optimistic, but on the other hand, why had he stayed?

"Hey, Ump!" Charlie yelled, so close to her ear that she jumped. "Want to borrow my glasses?"

"Charlie!" she said sharply.

"What?" he asked without looking at her.

"You don't have glasses," Simon said.

Charlie glanced down at him. "I don't need them. But that umpire does."

"He's been calling crap all night," Tom said without looking around. Charlie nodded. Malcolm had turned to see who had yelled. He waved to Charlie, who waved back.

Dave added, "His niece is on the mound for the Wildcats."

"Of course she is," Charlie muttered.

Sarah turned back to the field. She tried to pick out the pitcher for the other team, but she couldn't see into the dugout. Was it fair to let a family member work as the umpire? She supposed youth sports were like any other volunteer-staffed position—you took what you could get.

Over the course of the next two innings, Charlie offered the umpire his copy of the rule book, suggested that the man might want to keep his eyes open the next time he was calling a ball foul and was on his feet clapping when Lily knocked one over the left-field fence to score two runs.

The next inning wasn't going as well for her team. Cindi, the pitcher, had runners on first and third. Pete was out at the mound and Lily went out to talk to them, her helmet pushed up to rest on the back of her head.

On the next play the batter took a big swing and connected with Cindi's pitch. The ball sailed out of the infield and dropped into the empty space behind the center fielder. Lily ripped her helmet off and took up a defensive position at the plate, yelling for the ball. Charlie stood up and hollered for them to "Throw it home, throw it home!"

The throw came in at almost the exact same second as the runner. Lily kept her position, poised to catch the ball as the girl from the other team started her slide. The ball landed in Lily's glove with a solid thunk and Sarah saw her sweep the glove down, catching the runner's leg right before she was upended in a heap on top of the other girl.

"Safe!" the umpire called as the girls untangled themselves.

"What!" Charlie roared. He was standing up now, his voice added to Tom's and Dave's and Malcolm's and all the other parents' from their team. Sarah stood, too, anxiously waiting for Lily to get up. She felt a little better when she realized Lily was also yelling at the umpire even as she lay on her back, arms and legs sprawling.

Sarah couldn't hear what her daughter said, but it was apparently crystal clear to the umpire, because he jerked his thumb and said, "You're out of the game! Coach, come get your catcher."

Pete took Lily by the shoulders and led her away from the plate, but not before he murmured something to the umpire, who gave him a warning look.

The parents for their team had erupted into tense conversations, and scattered boos were drifting out of the stands. Charlie, looming behind her, looking murderous, kept muttering, "I can't believe it. What a terrible call."

Lily spent the rest of the game on the bench. Jordan Sampson took over behind the plate, but the spark seemed to have drained out of the team and they lost fourteen to six. Sarah helped Simon down from the bleachers and waited for Charlie. He'd gone over to the backstop. The white parts of his dress shirt were glowing in the dusky light, and his leather shoes and the cuffs of his suit pants were now covered in dust. She watched as he called the umpire over and said something to him.

The umpire got up next to the backstop as if he wanted to come through it. Charlie said something else and the ump pointed at him and yelled. Charlie turned and walked away, not looking back even when the ump yelled again.

"What did you say to him?" Sarah asked.

"Nothing," Charlie said. "Nothing that wasn't true, anyway."

"Charlie, he's a volunteer."

"Yeah? Well, he should make sure he doesn't volunteer for the games he's going to be tempted to cheat in."

Lily walked over, dragging her gear bag behind her.

"Hey, kiddo," Sarah said. "That was quite a play."

"She was out," Lily said.

Sarah was about to say something about the luck of the game when Charlie beat her to it.

"Damn right she was out. We all saw it."

Her daughter's face lit up and Sarah decided the lessons about taking life as it came could wait for another day.

Simon said, "Mr. McNulty bought me a hot dog."

"Gross. Pig hair," Lily said.

"It tasted good to me."

Lily climbed into the car and Simon followed her. Sarah turned to Charlie.

"You weren't very well behaved."

"Some things push my buttons."

"I thought you were always in control of your buttons."

"Yeah," Charlie said. "I used to be."

"This whole sports thing makes people crazy, but she loves it, you know?" Sarah sighed. "I guess I don't understand people who care that much about winning."

Charlie shrugged. "It's not always about winning. Sometimes you want to prove something to yourself. That you can reach your goals."

"She has a lot of goals."

"That's not a bad thing."

"I'm not saying it is." Sarah felt frustrated. "I just want to be sure she has her goals in perspective."

He was about to respond when Malcolm came up, hand out, eyes roaming curiously from her to Charlie.

"Charlie, you don't have a kid out there, do you?"

"No, sir," Charlie said. "I was just…" He didn't finish the sentence. Didn't look at her.

"Sarah," Malcolm said. "That was a tough call."

She nodded. Her heart was beating fast.

"Where's Erik?" he said next. "Isn't he usually here?"

"He had a meeting," Sarah lied. She didn't even know why she lied. She didn't like the way Malcolm kept looking at Charlie, but more than that she didn't like the way Charlie wouldn't look at her.

"So, what? He sent you instead?" Malcolm asked Charlie. "Getting his kicks ordering you around while he still can, huh?"

"No one sent me," Charlie said, his voice clipped. "I ran into Sarah and decided I'd catch a few minutes of the game. The Phillies are off tonight."

Malcolm raised his eyebrows. "So Erik doesn't know you're here?"

Goose bumps made the hair on her arms stand up.

Charlie managed a hearty laugh. "Someone had to keep that umpire in place." He slapped Malcolm on the back and then lifted a hand to wave to her casually. "See you around, Sarah."

It wasn't what he said, but the way he said it. As if he had absolutely no intention of ever seeing her again.

CHAPTER ELEVEN

THE AFTERNOON AFTER THE baseball game, Malcolm had stopped by his office. Charlie knew the man was angling for more details about what he'd been doing with Sarah, but Charlie couldn't have explained it even if he'd wanted to. What he really didn't want to do was talk about it in the doorway of his office, so he'd faked a pressing e-mail message and cut Malcolm off.

Kind of the way he'd cut Sarah off. When he'd walked away from her, he was doing exactly the right thing to protect his career, but he'd felt like crap. He couldn't remember ever feeling like crap when he was doing the right thing before.

He hoped she hadn't felt bad. Before he'd thought it through, he had dialed her number and she'd picked up.

"Sarah?"

"Charlie, what a surprise."

He was pretty sure she was being sarcastic, but he pretended he didn't notice.

"I'm sorry I didn't call after my birthday. I was—"

"Don't."

"Don't what?"

"Tell me something that's not true. We had sex. You

left in the middle of the night. You didn't call me. I didn't call you. That's the story."

He shouldn't have called her now. She was so unsettling. Why wouldn't she even let him tell a lie just to smooth things over? She was relentless.

"Charlie?" She sounded hesitant. "Did you hang up?"

"No. I didn't know what to say."

"You want to come over?"

"Come over?"

"Have a tryst?"

He sat down in his office chair. "Have a what?"

"Did I use the wrong word? Nooner? Is that better?"

He felt dizzy. He'd called Sarah because he felt out of control, but then she'd picked him up and spun him sideways.

"It's after two o'clock," he said.

She sighed. "So not a nooner, then. You're making this very hard," she said. "You can just say no if you don't want to."

"No, wait, Sarah. Give me a minute to catch up."

"Okay."

Neither of them said anything for a second. He was still trying to figure out how to get control of the situation again when she said, "Ask me what I'm wearing."

"What you're wearing?"

"Yeah, ask me." She paused, then said in a softer voice that made him think of her mouth and how it had felt to kiss her, "I like listening to you talk."

Charlie glanced at the door. Still closed. No one could hear him. No one would know what he was doing. Hell, he didn't even know what he was doing. But he cupped his hand around the phone and lowered his voice to growl, "What are you wearing right now, Sarah?"

He thought he heard her draw in a breath. He waited. Had he done that right? He wondered if this counted as phone sex. Did Lauren have the office calls tapped?

"My tiara."

"Your what?" The tension broke. Of all the things she might have said, he hadn't expected that. What the hell? A tiara? Like for New Year's Eve?

"My tiara. Want me to describe it?"

He propped his elbow up on the desk and rested his head on his hand. "No. Um." *Think, McNulty. What would a man who knew what he was doing say next to recapture the mood?* "What else are you wearing?" he tried.

"It's just me and my tiara at the moment."

His elbow slipped and he dropped the phone. So the tiara hadn't been sidetracking, it had been the main course. *Holy hell.* He scrambled under the desk to grab the phone.

"Sarah, why did you call?" His pulse was racing. All he could think about was her, her beautiful pale skin, naked and waiting for him. He imagined her in a big bed with white sheets and heaps of pillows all around, a ridiculous, but suddenly sexy, crown on her head.

"You called me, Charlie," she said.

"Oh. Right." He needed to do something but he couldn't make his brain work. "Just your tiara?"

"Uh-huh."

How could Sarah Finley, reliable, bubbly, always-your-best-pal Sarah Finley make two nonsense syllables sound like the world's most enticing come-on? Why was he sure she had one finger in her mouth? Why was he wasting time on the floor under his desk when he could be with her, in her bed, watching her tiara sparkle as he took that finger into his own mouth, as he let his own fingers…

Charlie was nothing if not efficient.

"I'll be there by two twenty-three. Two-seventeen, if I catch the light at Oak."

"The door's open, Charlie. Come on up."

He didn't even say goodbye. Snapped his phone shut as he was tapping his pocket checking for the keys. Sarah was waiting for him and that was about all he needed. He knew he should stop and think about this development but he'd made an appointment. Charlie did not like to be late.

Sarah hung up and ran up the stairs two at a time. She'd just gotten in the door from dropping the kids off at their cousins' house when the phone had rung. When she had heard Charlie's voice, it was a jolt straight through her. She'd wanted him to call, but she hadn't known what she was going to say. Then she heard his voice and she had a flash of inspiration, a way to get him to come over one more time.

She really liked Charlie, but she'd seen yesterday that he was probably not going to be able to give up his obsession with his career to admit they were good together. She would always come second, no matter what. She wasn't even sure they would be good together, really. Sure, they'd had fun almost every time, but those occasions were the aberrations in his life. He was a workaholic, career-focused, money guy. She'd already been married to one of those and she hadn't enjoyed it the first time around.

The fact was, she had no clue if she and Charlie would be good long-term because they'd never even approached anything like a commitment. She was sure that she definitely wouldn't be given the chance to find out—he was too serious about the partnership at work to commit to her. But she loved being with him. So when she'd heard his voice on the phone, she'd decided to see if she could get him to bend his rules one more time. She'd have one more memory with him. It wasn't going to be enough, but it would be one more than she already had.

When she heard the need in his voice, she knew she'd done the right thing.

Upstairs she grabbed a clean set of sheets from the closet and made her bed quickly. After plumping the pillows, she turned the comforter back. She looked around her room and wondered if there was anything she could do to make it look more seductive. But it was just her bedroom.

Cherry dresser, bookcase under the windowsill, side chair upholstered in black-and-white toile, sheer lace curtains under black wooden shutters. She'd painted the room Tiffany blue right after Erik moved out and bought all new linens in shades of gray, black and white to replace the mauve-and-green plaid and floral combination he'd insisted on. The photo portraits of the kids she had done every spring were framed in plain dark gray wood and hung in a grid on the far wall.

She pulled the curtain back and stared out at the street. He'd said he was on his way. How long before he would be there? The clock read two-thirteen. Ten minutes, then.

She remembered how specific he'd been. Four if he caught the light on Oak. Was she ready for this?

She looked down and realized she was still wearing her jeans and T-shirt. She ripped her clothes off, kicked them into the closet and shut the door before diving under the sheets. There. No worries about her bra this time. She giggled, then tried to compose herself. Giggling wasn't seductive. She should probably be on top of the sheets, but she couldn't manage that. She compromised by sliding one leg out and arranging the sheets high on her bare thigh. She leaned back on the pillows, but then she remembered the tiara. It was on her dresser.

She climbed out of bed, the afternoon air cool on her bare skin, and grabbed the tiara. She was just getting back into the bed when she heard a knock on the front door and then his voice. "Sarah?"

"I'm upstairs," she called.

Footsteps on the stairs and then he was in her room.

He had on another of his sober-suit-and-white-shirt combinations, but in his dark sunglasses, he looked more remote than she was used to. A magnate. Ruthless.

Her fingers twitched on the sheet as she quelled her impulse to pull the covers up to her chin. Maybe this had been a bad idea.

But he pulled the sunglasses off and folded them into the breast pocket of his suit. He came across the room, toeing off his shoes along the way, then knelt on one knee on the edge of the bed, his arms bracketing her hips, the buttons on the cuff of his jacket cold against the bare skin of her leg. He smiled, a sexy, dangerous, full-on predatory smile that made her skin flush hot then cold.

"I like you in a tiara, Sarah." He kissed her, his mouth firm and insistent on hers. "You should dress like this more often."

He loosened his tie and stripped it off while she worked his belt open and then his pants. He straightened up long enough to unbutton four buttons on his shirt and jerk it over his head. His T-shirt followed and he dropped his pants, stepping out of them to join her on the bed. She put her hands around his neck, her fingers rubbing the hair along his nape, and pulled him down to her.

"You know what I like about you?" she asked.

He didn't answer. His mouth was too busy kissing a path across her collarbone.

"I like that you have all these muscles." She ran her hand up his arm to his shoulder and then back down again. "But when we're together like this, you do what I tell you."

He murmured agreement as he moved from her collarbone back to her mouth.

"It gives me power. You know? I get what I want when I'm with you."

"Mmm," Charlie said. "Me, too."

"In fact—" Sarah shoved up and flipped them over so she could straddle him "—I'm seizing power."

Charlie looked up at her, his eyes unfocused. He blinked, long dark lashes sweeping down to cover his eyes. "What?"

"You have to lie still and let me do exactly what I want to you."

He reached for her and she pressed her hand on his chest. "No. You. Lie. Still."

He seemed to start to understand what she wanted because he dropped his hands back to the bed, flattening his palms against the sheets. He lay under her, his eyes tracking her, but otherwise keeping perfectly still. She moved her hands across him, tracing a trail from his shoulders to his belly and then down farther. She loved watching him respond to her hands, his muscles jumping and his breath catching when she hit a sensitive spot. She loved knowing that in this moment, she was everything to him. She was really starting to enjoy herself when he suddenly grabbed her wrists.

"Hey," she said. "You're not supposed to move."

He tossed his head back and pushed up under her. "Power. Right. But…" He closed his eyes and then opened them, as if trying to clear his head. "You're doing this wrong."

"I am?" She felt deflated. He'd been responding. Lord knew she'd been responding. What was she doing wrong?

"No. Not that. You're doing this right." He squeezed her wrists lightly. "I mean, you're seizing power wrong."

"What?"

He sat up and cradled her, their hands together resting between them. He lifted one hand and traced her jawline. "Sarah, you can make me feel anything you want. I mean, it's pretty clear I can't resist you, right?"

Where was he going with this?

"But the thing is, what you're doing is making me feel, frankly, amazing. But that's not power for you. You're still doing what I like."

"But you have to lie there and let me. That's my power."

"No." He raised her hand to his lips and kissed it.

"Your power is when you order me to make you feel amazing. Your power is when you say exactly what you want and I give you that."

She felt a blush steal up her neck. Order Charlie to…what? To…

"Anything?"

He shuddered against her. She could feel how much he wanted her. "Anything."

She thought for a minute, letting her body rest against his, teasing herself with the connection while their hands were still and caught between them.

She blushed harder when she leaned forward to whisper in his ear, but Charlie just smiled and in his whiskey-gold voice said, "You got it, princess."

He laid her down gently on her back, holding himself over her and the muscles in his arms and shoulders bunched as he controlled himself. "But I want you to know, I'm only doing this because you're making me. It has nothing to do with you being the most gorgeous woman I've ever been with."

Sarah closed her eyes, but then opened them again. She didn't want to miss a second of what he did next.

SARAH LAY WITH HER HEAD on Charlie's chest. She listened to him breathe. Her right leg was flung across his thighs and her arm was twined across his stomach, his wrist held loosely in her hand. He was so strong, the hard muscles in his biceps and chest contrasting with the careful way he held and touched her. She liked holding on to him and feeling the potential power in his body.

He was twirling a small piece of her hair around his

finger and then releasing it. The gentle, repetitive motion was soothing her to sleep. Every once in a while he'd stroke down the side of her neck with one finger. She relaxed a little more with each stroke.

He'd taken her tiara off and put it on the nightstand. The afternoon sun was shining through the crystals, throwing prisms of light on the ceiling.

"Where'd you get the tiara?" he asked.

"Won it in a poker game."

He slapped her thigh and she wiggled closer, hoping he'd do it again.

"Tell the truth."

"I was Miss Teen Southeastern Pennsylvania. First prize."

Charlie tilted his chin so he could see her. "What's wrong with that?"

"Nothing. Except I didn't really win. I came in third, but the other girls ahead of me all cheated."

"You were the only honest one in the bunch?" Charlie stroked her arm with his warm hand.

"The pageant world is a dirty place." She watched the sunlight dancing across the walls and ceiling, remembering how Lily had called the tiara magic. This afternoon was certainly proving that theory. "I heard Erik and Lauren are having a wedding reception," she said lazily.

His hand stilled on her hair for a second before he started stroking it again. "At the country club."

"Wouldn't it be funny if you took me as your date?"

Later she wondered if she'd said it on purpose. If there hadn't been some part of her that couldn't stand to be happy with him when she knew it was a charade, knew he wasn't going to ever commit to her. But at the moment, she honestly couldn't have said she meant anything other than a sort of stupid joke.

"That would be a bad idea."

His voice was flat. She didn't like the way it sounded. When he shifted sideways, moving out from under her leg and her arm to sit on the edge of the bed, she knew something was wrong.

"I was kidding, Charlie. Of course I don't want to go to their reception."

He didn't look back.

"They probably won't even have a band. Erik is a deejay guy. You'll be stuck doing the chicken dance and the conga to 'Hot, Hot, Hot.'"

He hadn't looked around. Didn't respond. She pinched her arm to make herself stop babbling. Charlie looked so tense, his shoulders hunched up in a tight knot.

"Sarah, listen." He leaned down and picked up his boxers, sliding them on as he sat, his back still to her. "We need to talk."

Oh, no, we don't. Talking was never a good thing right after sex.

"I'm sleepy. Why don't you climb back in here with me and we can take a nap?"

"Sarah."

She sat up suddenly, holding the sheet to her chest. "What?" she snapped. "What, Charlie? What do you have to say that's so hard you can't even look at me?"

He swiveled, leaning toward her with his weight resting on one hip. "You're mad?"

Men.

"You're making this big production about 'we have to talk,' as if I'm a complete fool and haven't noticed that we only meet up in private, that you almost choked when I mentioned you and me and the wedding reception, that when anyone sees us together you bend over backward to make sure they know you're not with me. Or worse, that you're babysitting me for Erik."

"Sarah, stop it."

"No. You stop it. I invited you over here for sex. We had sex. Now you can go back to your perfect life and leave me out of it. No talking necessary because nobody asked for your opinion. I'm tired of sex, anyway."

"You're tired of sex?" he said with one eyebrow raised.

"I'm tired of sex with you," she amended, kissing her immortal soul goodbye because there was no way she'd make it into heaven with a lie that big on her conscience.

"Are you breaking up with me?"

"I'm sorry," she said. "Were we going out? Maybe I should ask Malcolm."

Charlie stood and yanked his pants on. He grabbed his shirt off the floor and stuffed his arms in the sleeves and then faced her. God. He was perfect. Even fuming and with his hair sticking up in little tufts over his forehead, he was exactly everything a man should be. And she had to let him go because for him, she was nothing but a secret to keep under wraps, an obstacle on the way to getting what he wanted. She wasn't going to be that for anybody, no matter how good they looked in their post-nooner dishevelment.

He grabbed his shoes and his suit jacket off the floor. "This is crap, Sarah. I didn't promise you anything or take anything you didn't offer me first. Being with you isn't anything I ever planned on—"

She started to speak but he cut her off.

"I'm not saying I don't want it. I just… I need time. I need to… I don't know. I can't think."

"Nobody asked you to think about anything," Sarah said. "Don't you ever do anything just because it feels good?"

"No. That's not how the world works. Not for adults, anyway."

"I don't believe that. I did what I was supposed to do. I did every single thing I was supposed to do and where did it get me?"

Charlie shook his head.

"I don't know, either. So now I'm doing it this way. I like you. No one's getting hurt. I don't see what the big deal has to be. You can't be with me and make partner, I get that. But I'm not hiding out waiting for you to show up after dark so the neighbors won't see. Sex with you is amazing, but I want more."

"You're not listening to me, Sarah. I need to play this cool until I've signed Henry Ryan and I've got the partnership. I've been planning for those things for a long time. All my work, everything is wrapped up there. I just need time."

His voice was softer now and she wondered if she'd hurt him. She hadn't meant to hurt him, or maybe she had, but it didn't matter because what he'd said had just confirmed exactly why they couldn't be together.

"I do understand that, Charlie. I would never ask you to give up your goals for me. Can you see why I can't take the leftovers, though? After the Ryan deal, after Lauren and Erik, after your partnership, then maybe you'll have something left for me. I can't, Charlie…I won't be that far down your list."

He pressed his lips together and ran his hand over his face, rubbing his eyes. "So it's you or nothing?"

"No," she said softly. "It's me and what we can make together. I don't know what that would be, but it wouldn't be nothing."

"That's not what I meant," Charlie said. "The partnership vote is this week. I don't see why we can't wait. A few days."

"If you can't see it, then it doesn't matter, anyway," she said. "See you, Charlie."

He sighed, his shoulders and chest and head all slumping. "Bye, Sarah."

He hadn't been gone five minutes when Erik called. She blew her nose and tossed on a robe.

"Sarah, we need to talk about the meeting at school," he said.

"We need to talk about more than that."

"What do you mean?"

"I mean, you were supposed to pick Lily up yesterday for her game and you never showed up."

"Oh, God," Erik said. "Lauren had a dinner planned and the game slipped my mind."

She tightened the belt on her robe and walked across the bedroom to look at the portrait of Lily when she was six months old. She was sitting up on a fluffy white rug, but her expression clearly said "I'm above this." She'd walked early, talked early, taught herself to read when she was four. Lounging on a fluffy white rug hadn't been part of her game plan even in infancy.

"She can't slip your mind, Erik. You have to do better."

"It was one time, Sarah."

Which was an excuse she'd heard from him so many times during their marriage.

That was when it sank in. She'd been hoping all along that there was a chance he would be a better father than he'd been a husband. That wasn't going to happen. Erik was weak and he was selfish and he wasn't going to become someone else. Lily had been right at the game— Sarah had to commit to taking her to baseball because Erik wasn't going to do it. Not just baseball, either. Everything.

It was a relief, in a way. This wouldn't be the last time the kids would be hurt, she knew, but now that she saw him so clearly, she'd be more careful about their relationship with him. She'd do what she could to cushion the ways he'd inevitably let them down.

"Lily was hurt," she said simply. "Next time try harder."

"We really need to focus on the school meeting right now."

"I've decided that Lily can go back because she wants to be there, but I want to move Simon to the Ninth Street School. The program there will suit him better. There's more freedom in the schedule and the learning is child-centered."

"Absolutely not. Are you insane?"

She was surprised by how sane she felt. She picked up her tiara and put it on. "No."

"You cannot tell Henry Ryan that you've found a better educational alternative for our son."

"But I have."

"Simon's going back. Lily's going back. End of story."

Sarah took the tiara off and sat on the edge of the bed. The sheets were still warm and she got up, walking out of the bedroom, away from that physical reminder of Charlie. She couldn't talk to Erik when she was distracted by what she'd just lost. "That's not fair to Simon. You're setting him up for failure with that behavior pledge. He's been in trouble more times than I can count this year. He's not suddenly going to change, and the staff at Carol Ryan is not suddenly going to welcome him."

Erik was quiet. "I don't get him, Sarah," he said finally. "Why is he like that?"

"He's not like anything," Sarah snapped. "That school isn't right for him and trying to force him to—"

"Fine," Erik said. "At least if he leaves now we won't have to deal with him being expelled later."

Hearing him talk about Simon that way hurt her, but she hoped this change might ease some of Erik's tensions over the boy. If he wasn't worried about Simon embarrassing him in front of his client, maybe things would be better between them. "So we're agreed?"

"Make sure Lily wears a dress."

He probably thought he'd gotten the last word, but Sarah felt she'd won the points she needed. Lily could stay at the school she loved and Simon would get a second chance.

But when she sat the kids down on the patio that evening to tell them the plan, she got an argument from the one person she'd been sure would be happy with the arrangements.

"I'm not going back if he's not going back." Lily crossed her arms on her chest and pouted. She hadn't pouted in years. Lily argued rationally or stated her case, she didn't...

"Did you just kick the table?" Sarah asked.

"You're making me mad," Lily said.

"But you loved Carol Ryan Memorial. You told me you wanted to go back and I would be ruining your life if I didn't let you. Mrs. Camp agreed there would be no zeros. I thought you were settled."

"But I didn't know you were going to make us go to different places."

Simon hadn't said a word. He was sitting with his knees drawn up, his skinny arms wrapped around his legs, listening to them.

"All right," Sarah said. "I'm confused." She smoothed Lily's hair, tucking a stray strand behind her ear. "Tell me what you're thinking."

Lily took in a deep breath, her chin wobbling, as she swiped a tear off her cheek. "I know Simon's...well, you know, Simon. But...I'm used to him. And now that Dad's not here, our family's already split up. I like...I like going to school with Simon. If we go to different schools we won't see each other as much and he won't know my friends and I won't know his...the people in his class." She sniffed. "It will be all different and I'll hate it."

Sarah was floored. The kids had gotten closer during this month, but this was surprising.

"He can't go back to Carol Ryan, though, sweetie. It's not a good place for him."

"I'll behave. I will, Mom," Simon said. "I can. Lily, you'll see."

His sister studied him for a moment and then she met Sarah's eyes. In sharing that look, she had a glimpse of the woman waiting inside her daughter, the keen intelligence and generous spirit already well established in her girl.

"I don't think that will work," Lily said in a small voice. But then she looked back at Simon and said firmly, "We'll go to Ninth Street together. I don't mind."

Sarah had never been so proud of her amazing daughter. Lily loved her school, and she was willing to give it up just to hang on to Simon.

Simon spoke then for the first time. "Can you make that happen, Mom? Where we go somewhere together? Because me and Lily are a team."

"We're not a team," Lily said in a tone closer to her usual superior long-suffering sister persona. "You're just my brother."

Simon scratched his nose and nodded quickly.

"My only brother," Lily amended.

"The only one," Simon said in a goofy singsong that made them all laugh.

She had no idea how she would "make this happen." She could well imagine the fit Erik would throw. But looking at her kids, she knew it was time for her to figure out how to handle her life. She needed to stop reacting and start being in charge. She'd been saying she was finished playing by the rules, but she hadn't made new rules, just pushed back against the old ones. If she was going to be the person her kids needed, the person she wanted to be, then she needed to do better. Be better.

Stop waiting for someone else to tell her she mattered and take charge of her own self.

"I'm going to do my best," she said. She leaned out and took each of them by the hand and pulled them into a hug. She kissed their heads, savoring their warmth and knowing she would do everything in her power to keep them happy.

When they ran inside to watch a movie they'd been waiting for on the Disney channel, she stayed on the patio, feeling heavy and exhausted. She had so much to do, to be happy for, even. But she missed Charlie. She missed so many things about him. She even missed things they'd never done together but that she knew he would have loved. If only she'd been able to convince him they were worth a shot, but it hadn't happened. He'd picked his career, and while she understood why, it didn't hurt any less. She ached, knowing she'd been close again, but had come up short in the end.

CHAPTER TWELVE

CHARLIE SIGNED HENRY RYAN. It was two days after Sarah had said goodbye. Lauren took Charlie, Henry and Erik to dinner in the private dining room at the country club. The four of them ate steaks and Lauren made a toast to the beginning of a rewarding partnership. The way she emphasized partnership while smiling at Charlie was loaded with significance. She'd already told him the partnership meeting was scheduled for the next morning. He gulped champagne and did his best to look humble and deserving.

The toasting reminded him of that night when Sarah had her drunken breakdown. He wondered if the game was on at Wilton's.

"You should congratulate yourselves for hiring this young man." Henry put his hand on Charlie's shoulder. "I'm looking forward to a long and profitable relationship."

Which was exactly what Charlie should have been looking forward to, what he had been looking forward to. Until Sarah.

Erik touched Lauren's back just above the zipper on her dress, and she leaned over to peck his cheek. Charlie stared. That was what people did when they had something to celebrate. They got together with the people they loved and shared the good times.

He didn't think Henry would appreciate a peck on the cheek from him, though, and there wasn't anyone else to celebrate with.

He realized, watching Erik and Lauren, that this was it for him. He had hitched his wagon securely to theirs, and the promised partnership would make the connection permanent. Every time he went out with "people from work," it would be these people. Any time he had an event or an office party or any socializing to do with or for Baxter Smiley, he was going to see Erik and Lauren.

They were annoying, and the public displays of affection kept giving him visuals he could do without, but he could probably get used to them. But Sarah couldn't.

Who had he been kidding when he told her he only needed time? She could never, and would never, want to pal around with Erik and Lauren. The idea of anyone expecting her to want that was insulting. He wasn't sure if he'd been delusional or stupid when he thought he could strategize his way through this, achieving one goal at a time, until he ended up with the career he wanted and Sarah.

He lifted his Scotch and took a deep swallow. He couldn't change this now. He and Ryan had signed the agreements and the funds transfers were already arranged. As was usual, Charlie had mapped out his plan, knocked off each obstacle and achieved his ultimate goal. This table, right here at the country club, with Henry, Erik and Lauren, it was exactly what he'd wanted and now he had it.

The only thing different about this accomplishment, the only thing new, was that he did not feel the accustomed satisfaction of a job well done. He felt empty, and dumb, and so broken with wanting to be with Sarah that he couldn't even make small talk.

He excused himself before the dessert was served. He didn't have to make up a lie. He really did feel nauseous. At home, he lay in his king-size bed alone in his silent apartment, and stared at the ceiling most of the night.

When the sun came up he got out of bed and made coffee. He opened the curtains in his living room and looked out at the view of the river. His whole life he'd been running from the chaos in his childhood. He'd picked his career, targeted Baxter Smiley, cultivated his clients, even bought this apartment with its perfectly designed systems, all in an effort to make sure he would be secure. He had everything he wanted and he felt like crap.

He went to take a shower. The partnership meeting was starting in a couple of hours and he shouldn't be late.

SHE'D SPOKEN TO HER LAWYER the day before and he'd assured her that since she had primary custody and Erik had been skipping his weekends with the kids, that at least gave her strong footing to argue her decision should be final if he chose to take her to court over the school decision. She hoped it wouldn't come to that, but the only way she'd see the kids back at Carol Ryan Memorial was under judge's orders.

Her lawyer advised her to send a written notice informing the school of her intention to withdraw the children. No need to attend the disciplinary hearing when she had no intention of putting the kids back there. That's what her lawyer had told her.

She'd decided on her own that there was no need to inform Erik she wasn't going to the disciplinary hearing when it would only make him mad.

The meeting had been set for eleven o'clock. On the chance that Erik might show up at the house ready to take her to task, she'd called Hailey and asked if the kids could go over. She dropped them off around nine, and it turned out Jack was there having breakfast. He'd offered to take the kids to the zoo. Simon and Lily had leaped at the opportunity and she wasn't expecting them back until dinner.

With all that taken care of, she put on her tiara, dug a crowbar out of the garage, cranked up the Steve Miller Band's greatest hits, and set to work on her next project. Remodeling the kitchen.

THE PARTNERSHIP MEETING started at nine o'clock. At ten-fifteen, Charlie was still sitting in his car outside Sarah's house. His phone had rung four times; three of the calls came from Baxter Smiley's main line and then the final one from Lauren's cell number. He'd ignored them all as he watched Sarah's house. He'd been there so long he half expected someone to call the cops.

When he first pulled up he thought she was having a yard sale because there was a line of stuff on the curb, including an enormous silver chandelier covered in little medallions that were winking in the sun. There was a handmade sign leaning against a set of red leather bar stools that read "Free." Two people had already stopped, the first one loading up what looked like a box of white tiles and the second taking the bar stools.

His window was rolled down and the rock music pumping out of her house drifted in to him. There were occasional loud bangs from inside the house. He had no idea what she was doing. Which he was surprised to find was okay with him. Whatever she was doing might not be exactly normal, but it would be all right. Sarah had her own rules, but she knew what she was doing.

He looked at his phone. He could still call them. He could claim he was sick from the night before. They'd reschedule the meeting for the afternoon or tomorrow. He could have his partnership, have the Ryan family on his client list, have everything he wanted.

Except he'd stopped wanting those things. He wanted Sarah. He was just too damn scared to pull the plug. If he turned down the partnership, he'd lose the Ryan account. He'd have to start over basically from scratch at another firm. He could probably convince one or two of his clients to walk with him, but most of them would stay with Baxter Smiley—they were legacy accounts whose families had been with the firm for generations. No. If he turned Lauren's offer down, he was on his own. No plan. No fallback. No safety net. Just him.

And Sarah.

He sent Lauren an e-mail. Two words. No explanation. Then he was out of the car and on her front porch, ringing the bell and hoping she would give him another chance to do this right.

THE DOORBELL RANG just as she pulled down the cabinet over the refrigerator. The meeting at the school should have started half an hour ago, and she assumed Erik was arriving to have it out. She took the crowbar with her when she went to the door. Not that she expected him to attack her, but she'd discovered that she really liked the way the metal fit into her hand. Steve Miller was just launching into "Rock'n Me" when she opened the door to find Charlie on her front porch.

Her tiara slipped forward and she put a hand up to straighten it. He started at the sight of the crowbar.

"You're not Erik," she said.

His eyes tracked the crowbar as she lowered it to her side. "Sarah, I was hoping we could talk." He looked behind himself at the street. "Were you…" His eyes went back to the crowbar. "Were you expecting Erik?"

She smacked the crowbar against the palm of her left hand. "Yep. I was. Lily and Simon took the big knife to school again, so all I had was this." Her heart was breaking. Seeing him standing there and knowing he didn't want her was so hard. She hadn't had time to get used to it or to prepare herself. She'd be damned if she'd let him know that, though.

He surprised her with a huge grin. He was so handsome when he laughed that it hurt. "You planning to pry him open or just whack him over the head?"

Of all the things she'd thought of that might happen

this morning, talking to Charlie about braining Erik hadn't come up.

"You never know what I'm going to do," she said.

His smile deepened. "No, I don't, do I?"

She was tired of the banter before they'd even started. She couldn't pretend not to care. Why did he keep showing up when he knew they couldn't be together? "What do you want, Charlie?"

"To talk?"

She shouldn't. It was only going to lead to more heartache, but the way his voice gentled and his eyes softened, she couldn't refuse him.

"I'll turn the music down."

He followed her down the hall to the kitchen but stopped short in the doorway, staring around.

"I'm remodeling," she said.

The contents of her kitchen were laid out on white sheets in the dining room. The kitchen itself was full of dust and cracked plaster and broken white tiles she'd pried off the backsplash. She'd taken the chandelier down before she emptied the cabinets and put it out on the curb, free to a good home. The cabinets she'd pulled down were stacked near the back door, waiting to be hauled off by an affordable-housing group from the city for use in their own renovations.

Charlie put his head back and laughed. "You…you're remodeling. With the crowbar. And the tiara." He took a step forward, ticking the items off on his fingers. "I don't even need to know anything else. That right there, those three things are perfect."

The crowbar knocked against her knee. Her hands were

shaking all of a sudden. What was he even doing here? They'd said goodbye. Why was he here and why was he looking at her as if she was the only woman he'd ever seen?

He crossed the dusty kitchen floor in three strides and put his hands on either side of her face. "You're amazing, Sarah." He smiled, tears glinting in his eyes. "I'm an imbecile, but you're amazing."

She let herself be held for one long moment, relishing the touch of his hands, so sure and strong, the closeness of his body, the way he smelled of soap and laundry starch. But then she stepped back, pushing him with the hand holding the crowbar. "Stop it, Charlie. I can't do this. You have your life and it doesn't include me. You have to stop coming here."

SHE WAS ON THE VERGE OF TEARS. He felt like the world's biggest jerk. Why had it taken so long for him to figure out where he really belonged?

He was about to ask her for another chance when the front door slammed and Erik shouted her name in the front hall. He instinctively pulled her against his side, keeping one arm wrapped around her shoulders.

Erik and Lauren came into the kitchen in a burst of anger. "What the hell were you thinking sending a note? A note? When you knew Henry Ryan was going to be there?" Erik demanded. "The kids are going back to Carol Ryan Memorial and you are going to apologize to Ryan and you better hope he brings his account back—"

He broke off, staring at Charlie. "Where the hell were you this morning? We had the partnership meet-

ing, but you weren't..." His voice trailed off. "Goddamn it. Malcolm was right. You are sleeping with my
wife."

"Ex-wife," Lauren snapped. She was wearing a
tightly fitted red suit with gold buttons, and was hovering in the doorway, her nose wrinkling at the dust.

"Don't talk about Sarah in that tone," Charlie said.

Sarah slid out from under his arm. He wanted to pull
her back, but before he could, she was in the middle of the
room. She pointed at Lauren. "You, get out of my house."

She stabbed a finger toward Erik. "You, stop yelling at me."

Without even looking back, she slammed Charlie.
"You, stay out of this."

"I'll yell all I want. You humiliated me in front of Ted
and Henry Ryan. Ryan took his account and walked
after we just yesterday signed him. You have a lot to
answer for," Erik said.

Charlie moved toward him. "Want me to hit him?"
he asked.

"I told you to stay out of it."

"But he—"

"This is ridiculous, Erik," Lauren said. She took a
step forward and the heel of her black pump caught on
a cracked floor tile. She turned her ankle and fell,
landing flat on her backside. When she scrambled to her
feet, her suit was coated in white dust. "Damn it. Tell
her you're calling the lawyers and let's get out of here."

"Stop talking!" Sarah yelled. She put her hands out
and they all stopped.

"One thing at a time," she said. "Erik, I spoke with

my lawyer yesterday and the actions I took are within my rights. We can certainly hash it out in court if you'd like, but the children agree with me. They want to switch schools."

Erik opened his mouth, but she said, "No talking." Charlie wasn't sure if it was a coincidence or on purpose when she happened to smack the crowbar on the counter near her ex-husband's hand. Either way Erik stopped talking.

"Charlie, I'm very sorry if this has affected your deal with Henry Ryan. Certainly, if you'd like me to write him a note explaining the circumstances, I can."

"He's not my client. I quit." Charlie leaned back on the counter. He didn't give a crap if he got dusty—now that he was unemployed it didn't matter. For now he was going to enjoy watching Sarah take charge. He was still more than ready to hit Erik, might just do it at some point because the little twerp needed it, but for now he was going to sit back while Sarah took her ex apart.

"You quit?" Lauren squawked from the doorway in unison with Erik and Sarah.

He shrugged. "I sent you an e-mail. I copied Erik."

Erik pulled out his BlackBerry and started scrolling frantically.

"It just says 'I quit.' You don't have to read it."

Everyone was silent for a few seconds, the only sound Erik's fingers tapping the screen. Lauren let out an exasperated breath and strode into the mess. She grabbed her husband's arm. "We're leaving."

Erik looked up at her. "Do you know what he's talking about?"

Lauren tugged his arm impatiently.

He started with her toward the door, but then recovered his outrage. "This is not the end of things, Charlie. You can't sneak around sleeping with my wife and expect to keep your job."

"I quit!" Charlie repeated as Lauren and Sarah both said, "Ex-wife."

Lauren tripped again on the way out of the room, but Charlie barely noticed. He was too busy watching Sarah.

She waited until she heard the front door close. She had to hold on to her anger until she was sure Lauren and Erik were gone. She needed it to keep her strong, and right now she needed to be strong. She couldn't believe Charlie had lost the Ryan account over this. He must be furious. And to quit Baxter Smiley—what would he do without his work? She put the crowbar down carefully and met his eyes.

"I'm so sorry," she said. "I had to do what was right for my kids, but you got caught in the middle. I never meant to make a mess of your life like this."

He didn't look devastated when he came to her. He didn't look destroyed when he put his arms around her and held on as if he was never going to let go. He didn't look like a man whose life was over.

"Sarah, the only thing you made a mess of today is your kitchen. In every other way, you were magnificent."

"But your job. The Ryan account."

He smiled at her as he rested his forehead on hers. "I got the account. Signed him up yesterday and went out for steaks with the lovebirds last night to celebrate."

"You did?"

"Yep. And the whole time I was there, all I could think about was you."

"Charlie…"

He kissed her softly, his lips caressing hers, his touch gentle, but the charge it set off in her pulse was hot.

"I quit, Sarah. I'm officially unemployed, and I was thinking of asking you if I could move in here if I become homeless, but now—" he kicked at a stray tile "—I'm not so sure."

She wanted to believe that he'd come to try again with her. But she couldn't quite. Why would he? She'd gotten in the way of his dream and now he had nothing.

She backed up a few steps.

He started to reel her back in, his hands inching up her arms as his hips canted toward hers. She resisted. "Charlie, I'm not sure I know what you're saying," she whispered.

His hands moved again, cupping her elbows now. She let him pull her a little closer. Wanting this to be real.

"What I'm saying is, without you, none of that other stuff matters. I got everything I ever wanted, and it felt like nothing because you weren't there to share it with me. I want to be with you, Sarah, if you'll have me. I just… I was so stupid, Sarah. I can never tell you how sorry I am that I didn't figure this out sooner. I…just hope it's not too late."

His hands were on her biceps now, their bodies touching at the hips, the thighs, the knees. He put his mouth on hers again, whispering through his kiss. "I wish you would give me another chance, Sarah. Would you?"

She couldn't believe what he'd said. He'd given

everything up for her? He couldn't mean it. But she looked at his face, his eyes shining, hopeful but unsure, and she felt the way he was holding her, strong but close. As if she was a treasure he didn't want to lose. And she knew. She knew that Charlie wasn't afraid of her anymore, of what their relationship might do to his life. The only thing he was afraid of was losing her.

She put her arms around his neck and said, "Yes, Charlie. I'm in. I'm in for however long you'll have me."

"Oh, I'm planning to have you for a good long time," he said, his breath warm on her neck. "A really, really good long time."

"Promise?" she asked.

"Whatever you want, babe. All you have to do is ask."

Their kiss was deep and so hot Sarah was glad he was holding her, because otherwise her knees might have buckled. He walked her backward until he bumped into the counter and then he pulled her into him, taking her weight. They kissed, passionate and hard and she knew this was real.

He pulled back and stroked the side of her face. "I really want you, Sarah, but we can't do anything in this mess—we'd be liable to wind up with tetanus. What the hell are you doing?"

"I decided I want to be a contractor. I'm starting classes at the junior college, and this—" she looked around the devastation in her kitchen, the changes Erik had made half-dismantled "—is my first project."

He smiled and swung her around. "I love a lady with power tools." He put her back on her feet. "Can we go upstairs?"

She straightened her tiara and fluttered her lashes. "Why, Mr. McNulty, you're much too dirty to be invited to my boudoir." She grabbed him, smearing more dust from her hands onto his shirt. "You need a shower."

He kissed her neck and growled, "That is an excellent idea." She took his hand and started leading him upstairs. "Hey, Sarah, I don't have to go back to work today. Maybe we could take a bath instead."

Oh, Sarah thought. She could get used to Charlie McNulty. "I like the way you think," she said. "I really like the way you think."

EPILOGUE

Christmas, six months later

THE TINNY SOUNDS OF "Up on the Housetop" started again and Sarah laughed and lowered the camera. "JT, take the tie out of Tyrel's mouth."

JT pulled the end of his Christmas tie out of his son's mouth for the eighth time. Jack, Charlie, JT, Simon and Tyrel were all gathered in front of the slate fireplace in her newly finished family room.

"Hurry up and take the picture," Charlie said. "I have presents to open."

He'd been the one who searched online for four more ties to match the one Simon was so fond of. He'd made his dad and his brother wear theirs, and Tyrel's was looped around his neck with the ends hanging down past his chubby legs where he perched in JT's arms.

She managed to frame the shot with all of them looking at her and quickly pressed the button.

"Now girls, too!" Lily shouted. She held her tiara on with one hand as she ran to put her arm around Simon, the two of them leaning back against Charlie's legs. Hailey and Olivia joined the group, their paper-and-glitter tiaras festive even if the Happy New Year slogans were a little early. Sarah put the camera on the table and set the self-timer before she hurried to join the group.

Charlie pulled her in close to his side. Jack put one hand on her shoulder and she heard Hailey whisper, "JT, the baby," right before "Up on the Housetop" started to play again.

After the picture, there were presents and a family dinner. Afterward, a group of carolers rang the bell, so they all trooped out into the cold to stand on the porch and sing.

As the rest of the family went inside to dig into dessert, Charlie grabbed her hand and the two of them held back.

"Later on, after everyone's in bed, you want to play some poker, Sarah?"

The lazy, sexy way he smiled had her hot despite the low temperature. "You think you can take me, McNulty?"

He shrugged. "I decided to sweeten the pot this time, got a little something to raise the stakes."

"Charlie, if you bought me a thong, I'm not letting you in the bedroom."

He squeezed her ass. "I only wish I'd thought of that." He dug in his pocket. "Nope. All I have is this."

It was a ring. A beautiful square-cut diamond set in a wide platinum band with two sapphires nestled on either side. It was hands-down the most gorgeous thing she'd ever seen.

"Charlie," she whispered, "are you sure?"

"I'm sure. You win tonight and the ring is yours."

"Just the ring?"

"I'll throw in a guy who loves you."

"Sounds perfect. It sounds like a dream come true."

She put her hands around his waist and held him tight as she kissed him. "You have to win it, though," he said. "And no cheating."

"I never cheat," Sarah said before kissing him again and then going inside to gather the aces from every deck of cards she could find. She threw in the Old Maid from Simon's deck just in case.

And she won it all. They didn't even make it through half a hand, actually, but Charlie didn't seem to mind.

LATER THAT SPRING, Sarah framed the picture she'd taken at Christmas. Had it blown up to eleven-by-fourteen and made the store use archival glass. She hung it in the breakfast nook in her newly restored, back-to-basics kitchen. Every morning, before she and Charlie went out to the business office they shared in the carriage house, she looked at that picture and then at her family and she knew she'd won. They were all winners in every way that counted the most.

* * *

'THIS EVENING I'm flying to New York for two weeks,' Jasim imparted with a casualness that made her heart sink like a stone. 'That's why I had you brought here. I own this apartment and you'll be comfortable here while I'm abroad.'

'I can afford my own accommodation although I may not need it for long. I'll have another job by the time you get back—'

Jasim released a slightly harsh laugh. 'There's no need for you to look for another position. How would I ever see you? Don't you understand what I'm offering you?'

Elinor stood very still. 'No, I must be incredibly thick because I haven't quite worked out yet what you're offering me.…'

His charismatic smile slashed his lean dark visage. 'Naturally, I want to take care of you.…'

HPEX0110A

'No, thanks.' Elinor forced a smile and mentally willed him not to demean her with some sordid proposition. 'The only man who will ever take *care* of me with my agreement will be my husband. I'm willing to wait for you to come back but I'm not willing to be kept by you. I'm a very independent woman and what I give, I give freely.'

Jasim frowned. 'You make it all sound so serious.'

'What happened between us last night left pure chaos in its wake. Right now, I don't know whether I'm on my head or my heels. I'll stay for a while because I have nowhere else to go in the short term. So maybe it's good that you'll be away for a while.'

Jasim pulled out his wallet to extract a card. 'My private number,' he told her, presenting her with it as though it was a precious gift, which indeed it was. Many women would have done just about anything to gain access to that direct hotline to him, but his staff guarded his privacy with scrupulous care.

Before he could close the wallet, his blood ran cold in his veins. How could he have made such a serious oversight? What if he had got her pregnant? He knew that an unplanned pregnancy would engulf his life like an avalanche, crush his freedom and suffocate him. He barely stilled a shudder at the threat of such an outcome and thought how ironic it was that what his older brother had longed and prayed for to secure the line to the throne should strike Jasim as an absolute disaster....

* * *

What will proud Prince Jasim do if Elinor is expecting his royal baby? Perhaps an arranged marriage is the only solution! But will Elinor agree? Find out in DESERT PRINCE, BRIDE OF INNOCENCE by Lynne Graham [#2884], available from Harlequin Presents® in January 2010.

HARLEQUIN *Presents*

Bestselling Harlequin Presents author

Lynne Graham

brings you an exciting new miniseries:

PREGNANT BRIDES

Inexperienced and expecting, they're forced to marry

Collect them all:

DESERT PRINCE, BRIDE OF INNOCENCE

January 2010

RUTHLESS MAGNATE, CONVENIENT WIFE

February 2010

GREEK TYCOON, INEXPERIENCED MISTRESS

March 2010

www.eHarlequin.com

HP12884

HARLEQUIN® *Blaze*™

New Year, New Man!

*For the perfect New Year's punch,
blend the following:*

- *One woman determined to find her inner vixen*
- *A notorious—and notoriously hot!—playboy*
- *A provocative New Year's Eve bash*
- *An impulsive kiss that leads to a night of explosive passion!*

When the clock hits midnight Claire Daniels
kisses the guy standing closest to her, but
the kiss doesn't end after the bells stop ringing….

Look for

Moonstruck

by *USA TODAY* bestselling author

JULIE KENNER

Available January

---

red-hot reads

www.eHarlequin.com

HB79518

REQUEST YOUR FREE BOOKS!

2 FREE NOVELS PLUS 2 FREE GIFTS!

HARLEQUIN®

Super Romance®

Exciting, emotional, unexpected!

YES! Please send me 2 FREE Harlequin® Superromance® novels and my 2 FREE gifts (gifts are worth about $10). After receiving them, if I don't wish to receive any more books, I can return the shipping statement marked "cancel." If I don't cancel, I will receive 6 brand-new novels every month and be billed just $4.69 per book in the U.S. or $5.24 per book in Canada. That's a savings of close to 15% off the cover price! It's quite a bargain! Shipping and handling is just 50¢ per book*. I understand that accepting the 2 free books and gifts places me under no obligation to buy anything. I can always return a shipment and cancel at any time. Even if I never buy another book from Harlequin, the two free books and gifts are mine to keep forever.

135 HDN EYLG   336 HDN EYLS

Name   (PLEASE PRINT)

Address   Apt. #

City   State/Prov.   Zip/Postal Code

Signature (if under 18, a parent or guardian must sign)

Mail to the Harlequin Reader Service:
IN U.S.A.: P.O. Box 1867, Buffalo, NY 14240-1867
IN CANADA: P.O. Box 609, Fort Erie, Ontario L2A 5X3

Not valid to current subscribers of Harlequin Superromance books.

**Are you a current subscriber of Harlequin Superromance books
and want to receive the larger-print edition?
Call 1-800-873-8635 today!**

* Terms and prices subject to change without notice. Prices do not include applicable taxes. Sales tax applicable in N.Y. Canadian residents will be charged applicable provincial taxes and GST. Offer not valid in Quebec. This offer is limited to one order per household. All orders subject to approval. Credit or debit balances in a customer's account(s) may be offset by any other outstanding balance owed by or to the customer. Please allow 4 to 6 weeks for delivery. Offer available while quantities last.

Your Privacy: Harlequin is committed to protecting your privacy. Our Privacy Policy is available online at www.eHarlequin.com or upon request from the Reader Service. From time to time we make our lists of customers available to reputable third parties who may have a product or service of interest to you. If you would prefer we not share your name and address, please check here. ☐

HSR09R

HARLEQUIN® *Super Romance®*

COMING NEXT MONTH

Available January 12, 2010

#1608 AN UNLIKELY SETUP • Margaret Watson
Going Back
Maddie swore she'd never return to Otter's Tail…except she *has* to, to sell the
pub bequeathed her, and pay off her debt. Over his dead body, Quinn Murphy tells
her. Sigh. If only the sexy ex-cop *would* roll over and play dead.

#1609 HER SURPRISE HERO • Abby Gaines
Those Merritt Girls
They say the cure for a nervous breakdown is a dose of small-town justice. But
peaceful quiet is not what temp judge Cynthia Merritt gets when the townspeople of
Stonewall Hollow—led by single-dad rancher Ethan Granger—overrule her!

#1610 SKYLAR'S OUTLAW • Linda Warren
The Belles of Texas
Skylar Belle doesn't want Cooper Yates around her daughter. She knows about
her ranch foreman's prison record—and treats him like the outlaw he is. Yet when
Skylar's child is in danger, she discovers Cooper is the only man she can trust.

#1611 PERFECT PARTNERS? • C.J. Carmichael
The Fox & Fisher Detective Agency
Disillusioned with police work, Lindsay Fox left the NYPD to start her own
detective agency. Now business is so good, she needs to hire another investigator.
Unfortunately, the only qualified applicant is the one man she can't work with—
her ex-partner, Nathan Fisher.

#1612 THE FATHER FOR HER SON • Cindi Myers
Suddenly a Parent
Last time Marlee Britton saw Troy Denton, they were planning their wedding. Then
he vanished, leaving her abandoned and pregnant. Now he's returned…and he
wants to see his son. Letting Troy back in her life might be the hardest thing she's
done.

#1613 FALLING FOR THE TEACHER • Tracy Kelleher
When was Ben Brown last in a classroom? Now his son has enrolled them in a
course, so he's giving it his all, encouraged by their instructor, Katarina Zemanova.
Love and trust don't come easily, but the lessons yield top marks, especially when
they include falling for her!

HSRCNMBPA1209